WHITE BLOOD

Nanak Singh (1897–1971) is widely recognized as the 'Father of Punjabi Novel' and has left an indelible mark on various literary genres. He emphasized the interplay between character and incident, considering character as the determinant of events and incidents as reflections of character. His literary canvas often portrayed glimpses of contemporary life veiled in a shroud of romantic idealism. His novel, *Ik Mian Do Talwaran* earned him India's highest literary accolade, the Sahitya Akademi Award, in 1962. Additionally, his novel *Pavitar Papi* was made into a motion picture in 1968, and *Chitta Lahu* was skilfully translated into Russian by Natasha Tolstoy.

Dilraj Singh Suri, a technical writer and localization professional, hails from a family of writers and educators. Growing up, he was immersed in the captivating realms of novels, poetry, comic books and magazines, and it ignited his passion to undertake the translation of his grandfather Nanak Singh's epic novel, *Chitta Lahu*, into English.

WHITE BLOOD

Chronicles of a Masked Society

NANAK SINGH

Originally published in Punjabi as
Chitta Lahu

Translated by
DILRAJ SINGH SURI

hachette INDIA

First published in Punjabi in 1932 by Nanak Singh Pustakmala, Amritsar

This translation first published in India in 2024 by Hachette India
(Registered name: Hachette Book Publishing India Pvt. Ltd)
An Hachette UK company
www.hachetteindia.com

1

Print ISBN 978-93-5731-695-8
eBook ISBN 978-93-5731-879-2

Hachette Book Publishing India Pvt. Ltd
4th & 5th Floors, Corporate Centre,
Plot No. 94, Sector 44, Gurugram 122003, India

Typeset in Dante MT Std 11.5/16
by R. Ajith Kumar, New Delhi

Printed and bound in India
by Manipal Technologies Limited

FSC www.fsc.org MIX Paper | Supporting responsible forestry FSC™ C043100

To my parents

CONTENTS

Nanak Singh

An Introduction

NANAK SINGH (1897–1971) was born Hans Raj into a grocer's family in Chak Hamid, Jhelum (present-day Pakistan) and is popularly known as the 'Father of Punjabi Novel'. He lost his parents early in life and could receive only primary education. However, he never gave up his spiritual and literary pursuits. A musician's group that recited *Gurbani*[1] and performed devotional singing at Gurdwara Sri Guru Singh Sabha, a Sikh temple in Peshawar Cantonment, inspired him. Under its solemn influence, Hans Raj, who had already become a devotee of Guru Nanak, had himself baptized as Nanak Singh.

Thereafter, the genius in him came to the fore. He learned Punjabi in Gurmukhi script to read the holy Guru Granth Sahib. He composed short religious hymns praising the Sikh Gurus, encouraging Sikhs to join the Gurdwara

---

1 **Gurbani** is a Sikh term commonly used by Sikhs to refer to various compositions by the Sikh Gurus and other writers of Guru Granth Sahib. In general, hymns in the central text of the Sikhs, the Guru Granth Sahib, are called Gurbani.

Reform Movement[2]. This composition, popularly known as *Satguru Mahima*, first published in 1918, made him famous throughout Punjab as Nanak Singh Kaveeshar[3]. The book sold more than one hundred thousand copies.

A few lines thereof sound the extent of his dedication:

Ai panth de malaaho, kis taraf jaa rahe ho.
Hathhin pakar ke chappu kishti dubaa rahe ho.
Ki bhul gaye ho saake gursikh dharmiaan de,
Futt da shikaar ho ke jag nu hasaa rahe ho…
(O sailors of the community!
In which direction are you heading?
You are sinking your own ship instead of steering it!
Have you forgotten the sacrifices of the great Gursikhs[4]?
Becoming victims of the rift, you are entertaining the world…)

On 13 April 1919, British troops shot dead over one thousand peaceful protestors in what came to be known as the Jallianwala Bagh Massacre. Nanak Singh survived the attack but two of his friends were killed. This incident took place on the day of Visakhi – impelling Nanak Singh to

---

2 The **Gurdwara Reform Movement** was a campaign to bring reform in the Gurdwaras (the Sikh places of worship) in India during the early 1920s. The movement led to the introduction of the Sikh Gurdwara Bill in 1925, which placed all the historical Sikh shrines in India under the control of the Shiromani Gurdwara Parbandhak Committee (SGPC).

3 **Kaveeshar** refers to a poet in the Punjabi language.

4 **Gursikh** refers to the followers of the Sikh religion.

write the heart-rending epic poem, 'Khooni Visakhi', which condemned the colonial rule and unmasked the cruelty of the British government. He was only twenty-two years old when he picked up his pen to oppose their draconian laws.

The British government, on the other hand, was extremely concerned about his provocative writing. They immediately banned the book and confiscated every copy. A few lines from 'Khooni Visakhi':

Ajj fer oh vekh gulaam hoya,
disse tukre da muhtaaj satgur.
'Kaala Kuli' pukaarde hindiaan nu,
thhudde maarde naal majaaj satgur
Naale maarde fer na ron dende,
jekar roviye bhejde thaaneyaan nu...
(O Lord! Look! They [the Indians] have been enslaved once again,
How miserable do they look!
The Indians are addressed as 'Black Porters'.
They are kicked and treated badly.
They are not even allowed to cry.
If they dare, they are sent to jail...)

Nanak Singh participated in the Indian Independence struggle by joining the Akali[5] movement. He began editing

5 **Akali** (pertaining to Akal or the Supreme Power, 'divine') refers to:
- member of the Khalsa, i.e., the collective body of baptized Sikhs.
- member of the Akali Movement or Gurdwara Reform Movement (1919–25).

Akali papers. This, too, was noticed by the British government, and he was charged with participation in unlawful political activities and sent to Borstal Jail in Lahore. He described the savagery and oppression of the British towards peaceful Sikhs during the Guru Ka Bagh Morcha demonstration in his second book of poetry, *Zakhmi Dil* (Wounded Heart). It was published in January 1923 and subsequently banned within two weeks. He wrote his first novel, *Adh Khiri Kali* (Half-bloomed Bud), while still in jail.

'These developments brought much change in the writings of Nanak Singh. From a writer of songs in praise of the Gurus, he became a patriotic poet, raising his voice against the alien rule. He turned to penning novels of social reform', writes acclaimed author Sant Singh Sekhon.

Blessed with fame and inspired by Guru Nanak's teachings of universal brotherhood, this young Sikh in his early 20s had an awakening. In his zeal to preach what he had learnt and dreamt, he shifted to Amritsar, the Vatican City of Sikhs. Nanak Singh taught himself – besides Punjabi and Urdu – Hindi, Bengali and some English. From here, the pace of his work was incredible. In the remaining fifty years of his active life, he gifted the world, particularly the Punjabi language, as many as 40 novels and innumerable short stories and poems.

His epic novel, *Pavitar Papi* (Saintly Sinner), written in 1942, immediately won fame and literary acclaim as a classic. The novel was made into a successful Hindi motion picture, *Pavitra Papi*, in 1970 by his ardent admirer, Balraj

Sahni. The original Punjabi version is currently in its twenty-eighth reprint. It was translated into Hindi and several other Indian languages.

Nanak Singh wrote over forty thousand pages in long-hand Gurmukhi script. He was bestowed with many awards, including the Bhasha Vibhag Punjab Literary Award from the Government of Punjab in 1960. His great historical novel, *Ik Mian Do Talwaran* (One Sheath and Two Swords), 1959, won him India's highest literary honour, the Sahitya Akademi Award in 1962.

The abiding and universal themes of love, friendship and sacrifice found ample expression in Nanak Singh's novels. *Pavitar Papi* and *Ik Mian Do Talwaran* are distinguished by

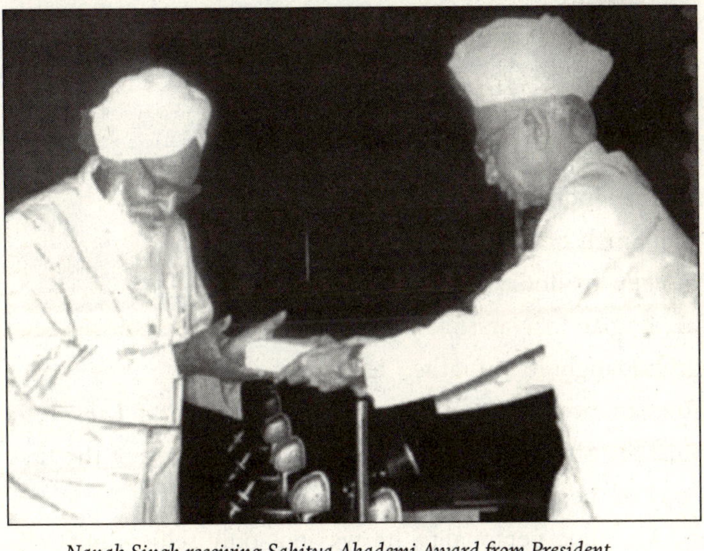

Nanak Singh receiving Sahitya Akademi Award from President Dr Radhakrishnan in 1962

the tragic themes of unrequited love and supreme sacrifice, while unmitigated greed and poverty were the themes of *Paap Di Khatti* (Sinful Income), which was also a reflection on the rapidly changing values of contemporary society.

Nanak Singh understood human nature, especially of the young and the poor, who were helpless and exploited by the selfish and the greedy.

He fearlessly pointed out the evils of fundamentalism and selfishness in our society, including those prevailing in gurdwaras and temples where many priests were dishonest, and some indulged in practices like consuming intoxicants and keeping mistresses. Nanak Singh revolted against these evils in his novels and short stories.

His centenary was celebrated in 1997. Such was his influence that to honour him, India's former prime minister, Inder Kumar Gujral, released a postage stamp in 1998. Former Indian President (late) Giani Zail Singh brought a copy of *Khooni Visakhi* to India from a museum in England. Natasha Tolstoy, the granddaughter of the legendary Russian novelist Leo Tolstoy, translated *Chitta Lahu* into Russian. She visited Amritsar to personally present the first copy of the translated novel to Nanak Singh.

A unique personality, he was not only selfless but self-effacing, too. Throughout his life, he shunned publicity and politicians. Even though he went to jail during the Gurdwara Reform Movement, he never sought to make political capital out of it. He did not even refer to it as a sacrifice. Nanak Singh was simplicity, honesty and decency personified. May we follow in some of the footprints that he, like other great men, has left on the sands of time.

Translator's Preface

CHITTA LAHU, ONE OF Nanak Singh's most renowned novels, was first published in 1932 and has since seen numerous reprints and editions. In this searing narrative, Nanak Singh expresses that the vital life force of our society appears to be diminishing, symbolized by the absence of red corpuscles.

The novel is significant where the historicity of Punjab is concerned and has shown Punjabi literature a new artistic path. While Nanak Singh had previously penned a few novelettes, *Chitta Lahu* marked his first major accomplishment, serving as a pivotal milestone that steered Punjabi novels towards realism.

The intricacies of Punjabi life, the distinctive qualities of the characters and their psychological depth are vividly depicted. Furthermore, the novel has been lauded for its well-constructed dual plot that is expertly woven with dramatic scenarios and irony.

Written in an ironical vein, Nanak Singh's seminal work is an effective satire on the society of the time. This peculiarity is crafted by him deftly while sculpting the different characters populating the story. It can be found in several scenes – the representation of the deplorable condition of writers; Rodu, the juggler's struggle for a better life for Sundri; preparation of illicit liquor by Pala Singh and his henchmen; a skirmish between the village Jatts over a scuffle at a place of worship; Anwarjan's dance performance; Sundri's meeting with Anwarjan and addressing her as Ma ji, thereby resulting in a dramatic transformation of Anwarjan's life. All these scenes are constructed with a brilliance that has never been found earlier in the history of Punjabi literature.

1

Unfinished Episode

'STOP THAT MAN,' THE railway officer said to the policeman. It was 7 p.m., and he was checking the tickets of passengers coming out through the exit gate. The policeman forcefully pulled the ticketless man by his arm and made him stand on one side of the gate. A bundle of rolled-up papers fell out of the man's torn pocket. He quickly leapt to pick it up and held it tightly in his hand.

The tall, fair Sikh passenger was not carrying any luggage and appeared to be around eighteen years old. His beard had not yet appeared. His shirt was torn at the neck, and his long, dirty black coat was patched in several places. Though mended several times, the coat's buttonholes had become too loose for the few remaining buttons to fit into, so he had passed thick threads through them to keep the coat in place and protect him from the cold. One of the pockets was completely torn. The man was the epitome of abject poverty and shame.

He began trembling as soon as the policeman touched him. Hundreds of passengers walked past him after handing over their tickets, but the officer did not look at anyone else as fiercely. To avoid the questioning eyes of passers-by, he moved two steps ahead and stood with his back to the gate.

'Oi, where the hell are you going? Stay where you are, or I'll beat you to a pulp,' the policeman warned him.

The passenger moved back.

After about an hour, when all the other travellers had exited, the policeman turned his attention towards the man. 'Hand me over one rupee and ten annas,' he shouted. The passenger was already searching desperately in his pocket. He pulled out a quarter-rupee coin, but it was a counterfeit. At that moment, he looked like a man dying of thirst who had only a small glass of salt water before him.

'Babu ji, please have mercy on me,' to he said in a trembling voice. 'I'm very poor. I tried hard to collect the money for the fare but still couldn't manage enough.'

The policeman laughed contemptuously. 'So, you didn't have enough money, but you still boarded the train as if it's your father's property. Didn't you think about landing in jail if you travel without a ticket?'

'We should search him to see if he's actually poor or just pretending', another policeman standing nearby suggested.

The officer agreed. 'I know this sort. They travel for free and waste no time in parting unsuspecting wealthy passengers from their belongings.'

'So, are you paying the fare, or should I issue a memo?' the policeman asked, glaring at the man.

The man's blood froze as a flurry of emotions flashed across his face. He tried to speak, but his voice kept dying in his throat. Finally, he gathered his courage. 'Babu ji, I'm guilty of travelling without a ticket, but I am not a rogue. I just have a bad luck. Do whatever you want with me, but for god's sake, please don't humiliate me', he said, his eyes glistening.

They listened to his plea without sympathy, having been habituated to the stories and excuses that ticketless passengers doled out. But when the railway officer looked into the man's face, he was surprised to see his wide eyes tearing up. His lips were trembling, and his fair face had turned red.

The policeman's heart was too calloused to be changed, but the officer found himself moved by the man's words.

All this while, the man had desperately held on to the bundle of papers. At times, he tucked it under his arm, at others, he put it in his coat pocket only to pull it out the next moment, fearing it might fall through if the pocket was torn like the other one.

'Come with me,' the officer said.

The man followed. Resigned that he would be taken to the police station, he was puzzled when the officer walked to a green lawn outside the railway station instead and sat down. He gestured to the man to join him.

'Where are you coming from?' the officer asked.

'Sir, from Lahore.'

'Where do you stay?'

'Here, in Amritsar.'

'And you don't even have a single rupee in your pocket? What do you do for a living?'

The man stayed silent for a while and then spoke softly, 'Sir, nothing.'

'Nothing? How do you feed yourself?' the officer asked. He looked at the man suspiciously, but the strange attraction in his eyes stopped him from saying anything.

'I don't know what to say about how I manage a living.' The man paused for a moment and then continued, 'Death is probably one's biggest fear in life. But god has made some people, especially people like me, selfish and stubborn, who want to live even after losing everything, even after all the disgrace and abuse.' His voice trembled. 'It's a real shame.'

'Be strong, young man', the officer consoled him. 'It's clear you're going through a difficult time. Let me see if I can help you in any way.'

The passenger was lost in thought for a while. 'This kindness doesn't seem right', he finally said. 'You should hand me over to the police so that I'm in jail before dusk... yes, that would be a better decision.'

The officer looked again into the passenger's eyes with the intensity of a jeweller examining an emerald for the first time. For a moment, he wondered if the man had lost his mind. 'How would this decision be better for you?' he asked, his tone reflecting his surprise.

Pointing towards the bundle of papers he was holding, the man said, 'I could finally finish my novel.'

'What do you mean?'

'Babu ji, I live in a tiny, poorly maintained home. The rent is only eight rupees a month, but even that small amount seems like eight hundred to me right now. I'm just an ordinary man who has recently discovered a fondness for writing. I've written articles and short stories for a few magazines, but this isn't my profession. Readers appreciate my work, but that isn't enough to do me any good. I've always been poorly paid for my work, and I can't make ends meet with so little.'

The passenger paused. 'A few days ago, when I was writing this manuscript', he continued, glancing at the sheaf of papers in his hand, 'I was as poor as I am today. I didn't have a single paisa, and nobody offered to help me. A day before yesterday, my stock of paper ran out, and I started panicking. Most of my novel had still not been written. I could survive without food, but not without paper.

'I was in despair. The never-ending poverty and depression were tormenting me. The drudgery was driving me to thoughts of suicide. I had almost decided to end my life, but the fear of leaving my novel incomplete… or, who knows, maybe it was some otherworldly attachment… held me back.

'While walking through the market, I spotted a used notebook in a pile of garbage. Maybe a student had thrown it away after using it. I picked it up. The pages were damp. Some were used on one side, while the others were blank. The notebook was smeared with ink, but I took it home and dried it as best as I could. It meant a lot to me.

'I wrote on those pages for seven hours continuously. There weren't any blank pages left to continue the next day, but the final part of my novel was almost complete. I was anxious to sell it and make enough money to fulfil my responsibility. What that responsibility was, and why I couldn't afford to delay completing the book further, I cannot tell you at this moment.

'I was confident this was among the best of all my previous works. I wanted to hand it over to a publisher in Lahore who values good writing. But going to Lahore without money was like going all the way to Calcutta.

'Yesterday, I somehow managed to borrow one rupee from a moneylender who usually gives loans to gamblers. He gave me one rupee but issued the invoice for two.

'This morning, without eating anything, I took my manuscript with the unfinished chapter and started the journey to Lahore. I thought once I struck a good deal, I would finish the remaining part of the novel sitting in a park, and then eat.

'I had thought I would read the entire manuscript to a publisher, leave a deep impact on him and get a handsome amount in return. But to my surprise, when I met the publishers in Lahore, they all looked at my manuscript like a bundle of garbage. Nobody offered more than ten to fifteen rupees. I was devastated. My purpose could not be served with such a paltry amount.

'I searched all day for a genuine buyer. I was afraid to return to Amritsar. I was dying of hunger. I only had a quarter-rupee coin in my pocket, so I went to a roadside stall and had only as much food as that amount could buy. But while paying, I was shocked to discover that the coin was a counterfeit. The stall owner threw it back on my face, and everyone eating there started laughing at me. There was no sympathy on their faces, only mockery.

'The owner shouted at me, like a policeman who had caught a thief red-handed. I had no choice but to part with my silk scarf as payment. Only I know how precious that piece of cloth was to me! It was the only thing remaining from my life's earnings. As I gave away the piece of cloth, the image of a loved one flashed before my eyes. I felt as if someone with tears in his eyes was berating me, "You, cruel man! Has *your* blood turned white as well?"

'Disheartened, I went to the railway station and boarded the train to Amritsar without a ticket. I started writing the concluding part of my novel in the blank spaces of some old newspapers, but I still couldn't finish it by the time I reached Amritsar. And here, I fell into your hands.

'Sir, this is why I'm asking you to send me to jail so I can finish the rest of my novel in peace. It's called *White Blood: Chronicles of a Masked Society*. Almost all the characters in the novel, except for a few, have lost their humanity; their blood has turned white. If you, too, who is now another character in my novel, had been selfish and cruel, the novel would have been an interesting tragedy. But now I'll have to think of a different ending.'

The officer was saddened to hear the man's story. *If the concluding part of the novel is so painful and heart-rending, then what would the rest of the novel be like,* he thought, looking at the passenger from head to toe with a mix of respect and sympathy.

'My dear man, forgive me', he said. 'I was not aware of your genius. Please rest for the night at my home. And if you don't mind, please be generous enough to read your novel to me. I'm very fond of reading and know a couple of local publishers well. Maybe I can help you get it published.'

The passenger silently followed the officer, who did not ask him any more questions.

When they reached home, the officer asked his attendant to arrange food for the man. After dinner, he gestured to his bed and said, 'Make yourself comfortable and read out your novel.'

It was around 9 p.m. The man pulled open the dirty string with which he had tied his bundle of papers. The haphazardly arranged sheets slipped out of his hands and scattered all over the floor. Quietly, he began arranging the pages. After some time, when all the sheets were organized, he took the title page and set it apart in front of him. The officer sprang eagerly out of his chair as if a senior officer had entered the room. Not much was written on the title page except these words:

White Blood
by Gupteshwar

2

GUPTESHWAR WAS NO ORDINARY name for Shyam Das. The officer had read his stories with great reverence and utmost devotion. He found peace after reading them and stored them as if they were holy books, wrapped in fine cloth.

Countless questions raced through his mind.

'Is this person really Gupteshwar? Am I actually sitting with the man whose every word is no less than that of a prophet for me? Why is he in such a miserable condition?'

He got up from his chair and sat at the man's feet on the floor.

'Are you *really* Gupteshwar? Are you the same Gupteshwar whose words are an inextricable part of my life?'

He jumped up and pulled out a bag wrapped in cloth from his cupboard. 'You wrote all this, right?' he asked, opening the bag. It contained a collection of all of Gupteshwar's works published to date – clippings of articles and stories from various magazines.

Other writers might have been elated at such praise, but the officer's words had no effect on the passenger. He nodded seriously. 'Yes, by the grace of god.'

Giddy with joy, Shyam Das tried to express the depth

of his admiration and respect for the writer. 'My dear Gupteshwar Sahib, I feel so fortunate to have found you today. I cannot tell you how much of an impact you have had on me. A few years ago, I led a hellish life. I indulged in all kinds of evil acts that I was foolishly proud of. But the day I started reading what you wrote, a drastic change came over me. I collected all your stories and subscribed to all the magazines that published your articles. The messages of universal brotherhood, spirituality and pain in your writing changed my life.

'I tried so hard to find your address and meet you in person, but I got the same answer every time I asked about your whereabouts: "No one has ever seen this famous writer."'

'Gupteshwar Sahib, some time back, this house was a den of drunkards, gamblers and drug addicts. And I was their leader. My heart sinks with shame when I think of the heinous crimes I have committed.'

Gupteshwar's heart melted when he saw Shyam Das's condition and how such a sinful man had reformed himself. He held the officer's hand and helped him sit in a chair. 'I'm glad to meet a fortunate person like you who has successfully saved himself from the clutches of evil. It is a task next to impossible, and I'm thankful to the almighty for having showered his blessings upon you.'

Shyam Das was filled with joy, but at the same time, he was ashamed of having disrespected the writer earlier. 'Please forgive me. I've committed an unpardonable crime today,' he said, touching Gupteshwar's feet.

'Sir, you are like my father. Please don't embarrass me by touching my feet,' Gupteshwar said, gently removing Shyam Das's hands.

'I'm sorry, my senses are not working right now.'

Shyam Das put aside everything else he wanted to ask and know for the time being and turned to Gupteshwar. 'Would you read your novel to me?'

'All right. But it's a long novel. You might get bored listening to it for so long.'

'Bored? There's no chance of that, although you might get tired reading it. I won't even have a glass of water until I listen to all of it,' Shyam Das said.

'Then you'll have to remain awake all night. I'll read it quickly, but it'll still take at least eight to ten hours to complete.'

'Even if you keep reading for ten days, I won't sleep.'

'All right then, listen.'

Shyam Das moved the overhead bulb towards Gupteshwar. 'Yes, I'm ready.'

Gupteshwar kept the title page aside and began to read aloud...

3

AS A DRY LEAF falling from a tree makes a crackling sound in the silence of the jungle only to disappear into that silence, so did the sorrowful cries of a grief-stricken young girl vanish within the pitch-dark cottage where she cowered on a winter night.

It was an abandoned place where men from the nearby fields came during the day to drink and do drugs. But no one dared enter it at night. The ill-fated girl was all alone.

She was around eighteen years old, her stunning beauty dulled by the shadow of immense sorrow, like a bronze utensil that had lost its shine after lying for too long in a smoke-ridden kitchen. She had dark circles around her eyes, and from her matted hair and tattered clothes, it appeared that the cruel fate had heaped her adolescence with misery.

The dark December night, with its looming storm and the sharp and rustling sound of dried trees, seemed to mirror her miserable condition. Though her body had been numbed by the bitter cold, the fire burning in her heart refused to be extinguished by nature's fury.

The night was passing as slowly as happy memories, but the storm grew stronger every moment, bringing the possibility of future sorrows.

Suddenly, the girl fell flat on her stomach, unconscious. Seeing her state, the stars closed their eyes, and the clouds began to shed tears.

The storm raged around the poor girl as she lay still on the ground. A strong gust of wind blew the roof off the straw cottage and tossed it aside. The walls collapsed. Some dry blades of grass gathered around her head for a while, seeming to shelter her, but like selfish friends, they disappeared when it needed too much effort.

Thick raindrops pierced her like arrows. Her thick, long hair, wet and heavy like a sinner's heart, whipped her back like the cruel stick of a heartless cattle herder.

Half-dead, the girl lay in the open with nothing to protect her.

4

HER BODY WAS WARMING up, and she felt some strength returning to her. Her eyelids fluttered. Slowly, she opened her eyes, but everything was hazy. She could not focus on anything in the dense fog. Her right hand moved, as if by itself, to the back of her head, her fingers trying to find the spot that was radiating pain. Her blood-soaked hair had matted, and a white bandage wrapped around her head.

Slowly, she regained consciousness and realized the condition she was in. A memory flashed, and she sighed deeply and fainted again. She woke after a while, and as she came to her senses, she realized someone was with her.

An old woman was holding her hand. 'Wake up, my darling,' she said tenderly.

The girl looked at the old woman but did not recognize her. 'My dearest girl! I'm so thankful to *Khuda* (God) for blessing you with a new life. I was worried about what Allah had in store for my child.'

The girl understood everything the old woman said, but the words '*Khuda*' and 'Allah' resounded in her ears a hundred times louder with the intensity of a loudspeaker. *Am I in a Muslim house*, she thought, her nervousness intensifying.

Had the woman not been sitting right beside her, shedding tears, she might have fainted again.

The old woman rested the girl's head in her lap and kissed her forehead, saying, 'Don't be afraid, my child, you are recovering fast.'

An old childhood memory returned to the girl. She was suffering from malaria. Her mother had gone to visit her parents but immediately returned when she heard of her daughter's condition. She had rested the girl's head in her lap with profound love, kissed her forehead and spoken similar words. She had recovered soon after that.

She felt as if that house, the walls, and everything around her, was her own childhood home. She was an eight-year-old girl again, with her mother sitting beside her, looking at her with affectionate eyes. The love of a mother, which she had long forgotten, renewed her heart as she revelled in that heavenly feeling, forgetting all her sorrows.

The girl gently moved back onto the pillow and resting her arms on her head, spoke with tears in her eyes.

'Ma, where did you go, leaving me all alone? Keep me to yourself. But Mama, you had died. People were saying that you died.'

'Yes', she said after thinking for a while, 'I remember, I saw Bapu setting fire to your pyre. And you…', she choked and started sobbing.

The old woman couldn't control her emotions. She placed the girl's head in her lap again and hugged her.

'My child, I'll always be with you, and will never leave you. May *Khuda*… God bless you with a speedy recovery!'

The girl sat up and looked around at all the objects in the house, including the old woman. Everything was different. The old woman was not her mother, she realized, but a stranger. The house she had thought to be her mother's actually belonged to a Muslim family.

'Where am I?' she asked, embarrassed and confused. Her mouth was dry, and she asked for a glass of water. The old woman helped her lie on the bed and left the room, saying, 'All right, my child, I'll just get some water for you.'

Returning to her senses by now, the girl got anxious. *She's a Muslim; how can I drink water from her hands?* she thought. *I won't drink it*, she resolved.

When the old lady returned, she came with a Hindu boy holding a glass of water. The girl felt her anxiety leaving with the drink of water. She asked again, 'Where am I? How did I come here and…'

'My child, I'll explain everything to you', the old woman interrupted. 'Do not worry. Think of this house as yours. We're Muslims, but we respect your religion. You're absolutely safe here.'

'I was returning from Ambala this morning with my son. My elder son works there as a contractor. We got off the train at 4 a.m. and hired a tonga to bring us home. We had gone only about a mile and a half when our coachman spotted you lying unconscious just outside Rihana village. We thought you were dead, but my son, who knows some medicine, examined you. "Amma, place your hand on her chest and check her heartbeat," he said. When I touched you,

I felt a feeble beating of your heart. "Let's hand her over to the villagers so she doesn't die from lying here for so long," my son suggested. But when we looked around us, nobody was to be seen. It was drizzling. We thought of going to the nearby village and reporting the incident to the sarpanch. But no one in the village would open their door at such an early hour, in such extreme cold. Most people are also scared of getting involved in such matters and being hassled by the police. Meanwhile, your condition was worsening by the minute. So, we decided to bring you to our home. The first thing we did when we got back was to call for a doctor. I changed your wet clothes and lit a fire to warm you up. Dr Gafoor arrived in a short while. He treated you for nearly two hours; God bless him! There was a wound on the back of your head, and your hair was drenched in blood. He stitched and dressed your wound and gave me instructions to care for you. You remained unconscious all day, and now, by God's grace, you've woken up.'

The old lady paused for a while before continuing.

'My dear girl, please tell me how fate struck you so tragically. Who is responsible for your terrible condition? But before anything else, tell me what name I should call you by?'

The girl's face betrayed multiple emotions as she listened to the old woman's story. At some moments, she was dizzy with anger; at others, her brow furrowed with hatred and jealousy; and, thinking of the old woman's kindness her eyes glistened with tears.

She did not reply to the woman's questions.

'Don't worry, my child', the old woman said. 'Even the best of us have to face troubles in life. No one can fight destiny. What is your name?'

'Gurdei,' the girl replied, wiping her tears with the end of her dupatta.

'All right, Gurdei, please tell me about yourself. Where do you live? Dr Gafoor is anxious to safely send you back to your parents as soon as possible.'

Gurdei sighed deeply. 'Ma ji. I'm very grateful for everything you've done for me, but it would've been better if you had left me as I was. At least, I would have been free of all my sorrows. But then, death is also scared of people with a fate like mine. I don't know how much more pain is waiting for me.' She began sobbing.

Moved by her anguish, the old woman embraced the girl deeply and tried to console her. When she felt a bit lighter, Gurdei began to tell her story:

'I'm from the village of Vairowal. When I was ten years old, my mother died. I didn't have any brothers or sisters. My father was alive, but he might as well not have been. He surrounded himself with bad people and ruined his life. While my mother was alive, there were fights at home day and night. Whenever she tried to stop him from drinking, he beat her mercilessly. She struggled through this living hell until she couldn't anymore.

'Bapu became a free bird after my mother's death. There were drinking sessions at home every day, and his drunkard friends clung to him like a shadow until they got their free booze. But when my father lost everything in gambling and drinking and became addicted, too, all of them vanished into thin air.

'I reached the age of fifteen when parents usually start worrying about getting their daughters married. But, my father did not care about me at all.'

'But why hadn't your marriage been arranged by then?' the old woman asked.

'My mother had me engaged to someone before she died, but my father broke it off.'

'Why?'

'What do I tell you? No one dared utter a word while my mother was alive. But the moment she shut her eyes, people started spreading rumours. Some said the boy's family rejected me for being illiterate. Others said my father must have asked them for money…'

'Why didn't they educate you, my child? Hindus send their children to school at such a young age.'

'My father was not one of those people. I was keen to go to school but he believed education corrupts girls. He used to say no one in our family had ever been educated, so why should he bring shame to our lineage.'

'I see.'

'First, my engagement broke off. Then all my father's drunkard friends showed up again, hanging around him and offering him booze they bought with their own money.'

'But, why?'

'They wanted Bapu to marry me into a family he was not

keen on. But who can fight destiny? They persuaded him, and a deal was struck. My father squeezed out two thousand rupees from my in-laws for arranging the marriage.

'I was married a few days later. That's when my sorrows truly began. When I reached my in-laws' house, I found that my husband was older than my father. He was an ill man, his health wrecked by asthma. The house was full of sons, daughters-in-law and grandchildren, and there was no shortage of riches. It was a wealthy family.'

'Bibi, your father did what he did, but why didn't anyone else from your community intervene and stop such a terrible arrangement – tying you to an old asthmatic groom? The worst is that he exchanged his own daughter for money after breaking an already-established engagement. How could everyone around him stay quiet?'

'Ma ji, you're talking about the community? They were the ones responsible for what happened to me. Those alcohol-soaked friends of my father were leaders of the community. If I start telling you all the stories of my village, it would take years to finish. If it weren't for their interference, I wouldn't be in this miserable condition today.'

The old woman put her hand on the ground and, then, touched her ears in prayer. '*Tauba*! What happened then?'

'That which was destined to happen. We were not married even for a year. My husband had asthmatic attacks almost every month, and the last one took his life.

'If my misfortunes had stopped even at that point, I would have been content. I would have spent my life like any other widow – in solitude. But fate had other plans for me.

'I had two stepsons. The younger one was unmarried and in school. He hardly interfered in my life. But the elder one and his wife had made my life hell even when my husband was alive. They started torturing me in every way they could. I'm a stubborn girl. I have a big mouth and couldn't stop fighting back and shouting at them four times louder. Maybe if I was educated, I could have been smarter in confronting them…

'I became a constant target in that house, blamed for anything that went wrong. No one treated me like a human being. At first, they expressed their hatred by hurling abuses at me, but then Karam Chand, my elder stepson, began beating me mercilessly. His wife further encouraged him.

'I couldn't even bring myself to eat on some days out of anger and despair. But no one ever tried to comfort me. At the end of the day, I would somehow force myself to eat.

'I continued living in that hell, counting every miserable moment that passed until the day I got the message that my father was sick. I was packing my bags to visit him when Karam Chand came to me. He politely asked me about my father's health and then said, "I don't think it's good to have this kind of hostility in the family. If you don't have any objection, let's meet with our elders and divide our wealth among the family."

'I agreed. After a while, he gathered some men from the community, including the village pandit. They had prepared a legal document and presented it before me to get my thumb impression. They told me what the document said:

"The total family wealth has been evaluated to be sixty thousand rupees. Of this amount, twenty thousand goes to Gurdei, twenty thousand to Karam Chand, and the remaining twenty thousand is to be kept safe for the younger son. Apart from this, whatever jewellery Gurdei and Karam Chand's late wife possessed is to be evaluated and divided into three parts. Two parts will be given to Gurdei and the elder son, and the remaining kept safe for the younger son's marriage."

'They got me to put my thumb impression on the document in the presence of several witnesses. As per their demand, I handed all my jewellery over to them. They told me to go to my father's house and that they would get my jewellery evaluated in the meantime and give me my share of the money, as well as my share of the property, when I return.

'I left at dusk that day. When I reached, I found my father struggling to live. He wasn't left with a single penny by then. His ravenous friends had sucked him dry. On my second day there, death came calling for Bapu. After attending his last rites, I rushed back to my in-laws' house. I was anxious to get my fair share of the property.

'I got there before nightfall. It was raining, and a strong wind was blowing. I was shivering with cold. As soon as I entered the house, I knew something was wrong. The lock to my room was broken, and it was emptied of everything. I felt like somebody knocked the wind out of me. When I asked what was going on, my daughter-in-law replied with venom in her voice, "Go back where you come from; there's nothing for you here."

'I was livid. I started crying and shouting. The entire neighbourhood gathered. Karam Chand also reached with the sarpanch and several panchayat members.

'Weeping profusely, I told them what had happened. My daughter-in-law took the paper bearing my thumb impression from the trunk and threw it before the panchayat members. One of them read it aloud: "After getting one-third of my husband's property, I'm going to the shrines. I no longer have any association with anything belonging to the house."

'I was furious when I heard that. But who would support me? Everyone from the family and even people from outside cursed me. After a while, when the outsiders left for their homes, I started crying. The elders of the house were on the verge of attacking me.

'When I finally threatened that I wouldn't leave the house without getting my share, they were further enraged. They already had the community leaders on their side. They started thrashing me. My daughter-in-law hit me so hard on my head with a *belna* (wooden cylindrical roller to shape and flatten dough) that I fell, stained with blood. They stuffed my mouth with a piece of cloth, dragged me out of the house by my arms and legs and threw me somewhere far away from the house.

'The rain was coming down with a fury. When I came to my senses, I saw that my clothes were soaked with blood and water. I struggled to walk back to the village and knocked on the doors of a few neighbours, but no one answered.

'At that moment, I decided to end my life. The simplest way out for me was to jump into the well and drown myself. I started walking out of the village towards the well. The storm was raging hard by this time, and the well was far away. There was barely any strength left in my legs. Taking even a single step was difficult. Soon, it was pitch dark, and finding the well became impossible. I tried to navigate using the frequent flashes of lightning. Unfortunately, I was going in the wrong direction. The storm was so powerful that for every step I took forward, it pushed me several steps back.

'At last, I dragged myself into a cottage, fell and fainted. When I woke up, I was here.'

5

EVERYONE IN THE VILLAGE knew Pandit Radhey Krishan, especially the young men who worshipped him. Some addressed him as 'Haatamtai' while others considered him an avatar of Vikramaditya. Whenever someone in the village was in a legal battle or involved in a serious family quarrel, they went to Pandit for resolution. And if someone was unable to make their way to his house, he dropped everything and rushed to offer them a solution.

Once, when a villager's buffalo entered Lala Bhaane Shah's fields and ruined his crop, Pandit helped him file a legal case against the man to recover the damages. The villager, unaware of Pandit's reputation, started arguing with him. That's when Pandit's curse fell upon the man, and misfortunes assailed him. Even six years after that incident, he was unable to repay his debt. He even had to sell all his cattle, yet Bhaane Shah's debt remained unpaid.

Pandit's devotees repeatedly narrated these stories to the villagers over the years, convincing them that he was a saint with otherworldly powers. But Pandit's biggest miracle seemed to be that he did not do any work or even read horoscopes and yet led a life of wealth. He had kicked his wife out of the house, accusing her of being immoral and wicked. He disliked the fact that she regularly distributed half of their food among the poor and that despite being his wife, she was unable to assert her position among the rich women of the village and collect charity from them. The moment she heard about someone in distress, she rushed to help them with even the most menial task they needed. One day, Pandit said he had received a message from god that his wife was a shudra in her last birth, and since then, he had completely ignored her existence.

Pandit was a compelling speaker and had a deep knowledge of oral scriptures. Despite never touching a holy book, he had mastered them and knew more about them than even the most avid reader. His success and popularity came from inspiring people to practise what he called the 'forgotten' divine teachings. He urged the villagers to recall that opium was associated with Lord Shiva and encouraged them to use it. He called alcohol the 'fourteenth *ratna*' of the gods. He enticed the villagers to gamble, citing it as the favourite pastime of Kauravas and Pandavas. The great Pandit had exploited countless people in a single lifetime.

When wealthy young men from the city thronged Pandit's gurukul, he took on the role of a politician, spoke on social and political issues and enraptured his audience.

It was 8 p.m. one night. Winter was at its peak, but even that did not dim Pandit's radiance. Bright red coals burned in the brazier, and the chill dared not enter his home. His assistants were preparing some of the finest delicacies for the dinner. Alam, the adept fish cook in Khwaja Sahib's household, was especially included as part of the culinary team. Warmed by alcohol, the cold wave was far from the minds and bodies of Pandit's inebriated followers.

By 9 p.m., all his followers had taken their seats. Pandit positioned himself gracefully on his throne amidst a standing ovation. One of his followers opened a liquor bottle, arranged all the dishes and sought his approval to commence the feast.

He looked at his followers with benevolence. 'Friends! Please wait a while. Let Khwaja Sahib, the jewel of our congregation, arrive first. Has anyone invited him?'

'Ji, I went to his place twice', one of the followers replied. 'He was ready to leave when two unknown villagers came to meet him. That's probably the reason for his delay.'

Hearing the sound of heavy footsteps, Pandit said, 'He has come.' He quickly got up from his throne and walked to the entrance to receive his honoured guest.

Khwaja Sher Khan, sub-inspector of the police department, had been working in the area for almost three years. Pandit welcomed him warmly, and both of them took their seats.

'We've been desperately waiting for you, sir. A few minutes more, and we would have cancelled this gathering. After all, how can the troops celebrate without their commander?' Pandit said.

Flattered, Khwaja Sahib adjusted the pleats of his majestic turban. 'I'm overwhelmed, Panditji! Mashallah, how could I not attend? I would've arrived on time if it wasn't something urgent.'

'Did you catch any new fish?' Pandit whispered in Khwaja Sahib's ear, moving a little closer.

'Yes, *Khuda* sent a benefactor to me.' Removing his turban and handing it to one of the followers, Khwaja Sahib rubbed his hand over his bald head.

'Did they make it worth your while? What was the matter?'

'It wasn't anything big.'

'Ah, I thought maybe it was something like a murder case.'

'No, Pandit ji, no such fortune this time. That's only once or twice a year. If we got murder cases every day, wouldn't we be eating with golden spoons right now?'

'Still, it must have been worth four or five hundred?'

'No, only two hundred.'

'What was it about?'

'It was Jatts from the neighbouring village of Sultanpur. They were on their way to court, expecting a verdict in their favour.'

'That means they've prayed for something good. If everything works out, I'm sure they'll stuff your pockets too.'

'I hope so.'

'That's good. We must thank God. He provides us with the means for a good living one way or another. Allah is great. He provides food even to worms living under a rock. You must be aware of the reason for today's gathering and of your host, Karam Chand. He is a magnanimous man, Khwaja Sahib! I had a very good relationship with his father when he was alive. He was a real gentleman, too.'

Khwaja Sahib smiled at Karam Chand, who instantly bowed with his hands pressed together. Khwaja Sahib gestured at him to sit down. 'This is about that young girl Gurdei, isn't it? I'm aware of the case, Pandit ji. It's good that she got kicked out of the village. Does anyone know where she is now?'

'I don't know for sure yet, but a reliable source told me that he saw a burqa-clad woman take her away in a tonga. A young man was with her', Pandit said while offering a drink to Khwaja Sahib.

'What? A Muslim?' Khwaja Sahib asked, gulping it down in one shot.

'Yes, Khwaja Sahib. I saw the tonga carrying them past my fields', the village gloss, Jwala Singh, chimed in.

Khwaja Sahib felt the warm glow of the second drink coursing through his body. 'Forget about all that now. Whatever happened was good. Let's just enjoy the party now.'

He didn't need to ask again. Bottles were promptly opened, and glasses drained.

'Khwaja Sahib, your cook is an expert in making fish. It's so delicious, I can't stop eating,' Pandit said, pulling a bone out from a piece of fish.

'He's been with me for five years now. His father, God bless him, was so good that he worked in Major Burlton's kitchen for four years.'

'Friends!' Pandit shouted jubilantly, demanding the attention of his inebriated audience. 'What a blessed time this is! There is the true spirit of national integration and universal love here tonight. Whenever I see Hindus and Muslims eating, drinking and celebrating together, my heart is filled with tremendous joy. May God bless all of India with this spirit!'

'Pandit ji! I swear by *Khuda*, all this prosperity is because of the power of alcohol. It really is one of the best divine treasures. Don't non-drinkers know how powerful it is in strengthening the bond of love?' Khwaja Sahib said.

'Those damn fools don't know the true meaning of friendship. Sahib! I just remembered. You've expressed your desire many times, and today, I'm going to present something special in your service.'

'What's that?'

'Your favourite home brew.'

Pandit turned to his follower, Piara Singh. 'Go to Jwala Singh's house and get that special brew you always insisted on presenting to Khwaja Sahib. Go, bring it quickly.'

'At your service, sir,' Piara Singh said. He nudged his cousin Dhanna Singh, who was drunkenly swaying next to him. 'Listen carefully, Dhanna, run to your home and ask your sister-in-law to open the door of the cattle-feed store. Go inside, and on your left, you will find a small pitcher kept under a pile of wooden sticks. It's covered with a big round container with a thick coating of wheat flour. Get it carefully, and don't spill anything inside. Go quickly now, my brother, and return with the pitcher immediately.'

The young man returned shortly with the pitcher of homemade liquor and placed it in front of Khwaja Sahib. The sub-inspector, who had started feeling tired by then, jumped in excitement when he saw it. He dipped his fingers in the pitcher and licked them. Pleased by the taste, he filled his glass and started drinking.

'What a delightful drink!'

'Didn't I say so?' Pandit said.

'Why didn't you call for it before?'

'I was hesitant because of your status and position. Otherwise…'

'Pandit ji! How can you say that? You're like my brother. Enough, enough,' he said as another glass was filled. 'There's no doubt this is magnificent.'

The party raged till midnight. What everyone's condition was by the end and how they got back home is anyone's guess.

6

DUSK HAD SPREAD ITS wings of darkness. A tonga halted at the village bus stop. A young man got off and, stopping a passerby, asked, 'Excuse me, could you please tell me the way to Pandit Radhey Krishan's house?'

'Over there,' he replied, pointing at a bungalow. 'What work do you have with him?'

'We need to meet him for something urgent', the young man said, looking at the girl sitting inside the tonga.

He walked up to her. 'Come, *behen* ji, let me take you to Pandit's house.'

The girl stepped out and followed the young man without saying a word. They reached Pandit's house, and the young man knocked at the door. A thin boy opened it. 'Yes, what is it?' he asked.

'I want to meet Pandit ji.'

'He is busy with his prayers.'

'It's okay, we'll wait for him. When will he be free to meet us?'

'In an hour,' the boy said and went back inside.

Forty-five minutes later, Pandit came out. The young man sprang to his feet to greet him.

'Stand a little away from the door!' Pandit said. 'This is a brahmin's house.'

'Sorry, Pandit ji,' the young man replied, flushed with embarrassment. Gesturing at the girl, he continued, 'I found her lying unconscious on the outskirts of the village early morning yesterday. My *walida* (mother) and I noticed her miserable condition and brought her to our village as we couldn't find anybody around at that time. By Allah's grace, she's better. She told us that she is the widow of Lala Mitha Mal. Please talk to her and, if possible, please help her reconcile with her family. I'll be very grateful to you.'

'*Behen* ji, please tell Pandit ji what happened to you', the young man asked the girl.

Pandit's face reddened with anger as he heard him speak.

'You seem to be an educated young man, but you are completely illiterate.'

Astonished, the young man replied, '*Banda Nawaz*, compared to the knowledge of someone such as you, I am certainly an illiterate, even though I am a graduate. If I have said something wrong by mistake, I apologize.'

'I understand now,' Pandit laughed. 'Educated people like you have ruined our country. If you weren't so educated, you would not have dared call this girl "*behen* ji" or made her sit next to you in a tonga, or even taken her to your home and tarnished her life.'

Confounded by this reaction, the young man stayed quiet for a while. 'I beg your pardon,' he finally said, 'but I implore you to arrange to send this poor girl to her family.

We have heard her story in her own words, and she has suffered a lot.'

'No!' Pandit said sternly. 'She has fallen from the Hindu faith. There is no way that she...' He paused suddenly and bit his finger, thinking. 'But of course, I do pity her miserable condition,' he continued in a softer voice. 'Ever since I heard she was kicked out of her house by her stepsons, I haven't been able to eat.'

'My child,' he said, turning to Gurdei, 'please make yourself comfortable here. I'll call those scoundrels here and teach them a lesson. Don't worry, everything will be okay. *Hari Om.*'

The young man was overwhelmed by Pandit's sudden transformation from anger to kindness. He bent down to touch his feet. 'You really are a nobleman, and I'm—'

Pandit quickly took three steps back. 'Don't touch my feet! I'll have to take another bath on such a cold day.'

Embarrassed again, the young man stepped back and saluted him from a distance. He turned to Gurdei. 'Goodbye, *behen*—' he was about to say when he realized his mistake. Without another word, he sat down in the tonga and rode off. Gurdei watched till he disappeared from view, her eyes moist with gratitude.

When she went inside, Pandit was returning to his prayer room. 'Sit on this stool, my child. I'll be right back after finishing my meditation. *Hari Om.*'

She sat down on the floor, squeezing herself into a corner.

Pandit was soon lost in prayer. After several minutes

of chanting, he counted his beads in front of a cow-faced sculpture for a long time. Finally, he sat on the bed near Gurdei.

'Yes, my child. What do you want to say?'

Gurdei stayed quiet for a while, absently digging at the floor with a stick. 'Pandit ji, nothing is hidden from you,' she finally said softly, her head bowed.

Moving his hand to his belly, Pandit belched and followed it with a dragged '*Hari Om*.'

'Yes, my servant, Raja Ram, told me last night that Karam Chand had kicked you out of his house after beating you badly. I was deep in my daily meditation, so I couldn't get enough time to see what was happening.'

'Pandit ji, perhaps you don't remember,' Gurdei said shyly, 'you were standing near Karam Chand and whispering something to him.'

Pandit's forehead twitched.

'*Shiv*! *Shiv*! My memory has become so weak. I couldn't even tell you what I ate for dinner last night. I remember now. I was carrying some supplies for my prayers back from the market and heard loud noises from your house. I decided to intervene and resolve whatever the issue was. I told Karam Chand not to commit such atrocities and told him to give you the appropriate share that you rightfully deserve. But that monster didn't listen to anyone. What happened afterwards?'

Gurdei told him the story of her suffering. As she spoke about the kind-heartedness of Abdul Gaffoor and his mother, Pandit grew furious. Biting his lip, he hissed, 'My child! You don't understand how evil the intentions of these people are. They have desecrated your religion. Who knows to what extent? My heart sank when I found out that a Muslim had carried you away while you were unconscious. A Muslim family tormenting a Hindu girl! I ordered one of my servants to rush to their place with a tonga to bring you back. That's why that bastard dropped you here peacefully.' He hiccupped loudly, '*Hari Om*.'

Gurdei was upset with Pandit's explanation. She wanted to speak but paused. Restraining herself, she said instead, 'Yes, I had asked them to do so.'

'What?'

'I had asked them to bring me here instead of taking me to my house. I thought you would be able to help me.'

'Ah, so you asked them, and my message reached them, too. Obviously, they had to send you to my place. Anyway, tell me, what do you want me to do?'

'Please help me get my share.'

'What if you live with them like you used to?'

'They won't let me stay there even for a moment.'

'Hmm. Go and sit in the room upstairs; I'll call them right now,' Pandit said, his mind working furiously.

Gurdei bowed her head and went upstairs. Pandit wore his robes and walked out.

7

A MEETING OF THE panchayat heads was soon held at Karam Chand's house, presided over by Pandit.

Chowdhry Ditta Mal put a hookah pipe in his mouth and blew out a stream of smoke. 'Karam Chand, what happened with your issue, finally?' he asked, coughing.

Karam Chand scratched his turban. 'Chowdhry ji, everything happened in front of your eyes. But Pandit ji has fresh news for us.'

The pandit belched, '*Hari Om*,' he intoned.

'Chowdhry ji, what is there left to say? These are bad times. I pray every morning and evening before the Almighty not to abandon me. Life has been peaceful so far, and I wish it would remain the same for whatever is left. Instead of making me participate in such profane activities, I wish God would take me away from this earth. But who can say what is in store for us?'

Bursting with curiosity about his news, a chorus of voices surrounded him. 'Tell us, Maharaj, tell us.'

'What am I supposed to tell you?' Pandit snarled. 'It is the result of your own misdeeds. You've turned away from prayer and meditation and indulged in sinful behaviour. You are causing chaos in our community.' After a moment of silence, he looked at Karam Chand. 'I've been telling you since long to rein in that damn girl. And now, look. What I was afraid of has happened. That cursed girl landed herself with a Muslim family. I swear by God, my blood has been boiling since I heard about it. If such heinous things happen in our village in front of our eyes, then we may as well be cursed.' *Hic*. '*Hari Om*.' The group was in awe of Pandit's piety and wisdom. They broke out into a new chorus, extolling his greatness.

Pandit spoke to Karam Chand and Mohan Lal, 'The young men of today have lost their way. They are aberrations. They stink of selfishness. You idiots! You should have at least consulted me once. This brahmin is not your enemy. I was raised by *your* elders. Even if I was incapable of giving you good advice, I wouldn't have given you any bad advice at least. But you don't care. Enjoy yourself, do whatever you want. Who am I to interfere in your personal matters?' He placed his hands on his knees, attempting to stand up and leave.

Panicked, the men gathered around him. 'No, Maharaj, please be seated, listen to us, why are you getting angry…' One of them placed his head at Pandit's feet, one took his walking stick away from his hand, and another stood in front of him.

The helpless Pandit had to remain seated. Holding a muffler in both hands, Karam Chand bowed at his feet and pleaded, 'Maharaj! Our honour is in your hands. Please counsel us on this issue, otherwise, the community will make our life a living hell.'

'Yes, Maharaj, this poor man is being harassed everywhere,' somebody else added.

Among the group was Mohan Lal, son of Munshi Devi Dayal. He had recently finished his studies and returned to the village. 'Pandit ji, this is without a doubt a noble cause,' he said. 'Only a learned man like you can resolve such a complex problem. That poor girl can still come back home if you try.'

'What did you say? She can come back?' Pandit spluttered. He looked at the village heads. 'Have you heard this moron?' He turned back to the young man. 'Is this what the Aryans have taught you? Think before you speak, and don't interrupt the discussions of your elders. It's like an illiterate arguing among intellectuals.'

Everyone glared at Mohan Lal, cursing him for his audacity. But the young man could not stay quiet. 'I beg your pardon, Pandit ji, but I didn't say anything wrong. What is the harm if the poor girl is allowed to return to the community? She is a child widow. If Lala Karam Chand is unable to look after her, then she could be allowed to marry a suitable—'

Pandit's anger erupted. 'Enough! Don't you dare utter such filthy words again. Can a donkey be turned into a cow just by cleaning thoroughly? Don't you feel ashamed about disgracing our faith by suggesting that widows should remarry?' Slapping his palms on his forehead, he continued, 'This is sickening, my friends. These Aryans and Akalis have corrupted Indian culture.' *Hic*. '*Hari Om*.'

'All right, Pandit ji', Mohan Lal said, 'As per your own words, if a fool cannot be an intellectual, then how can an intellectual be a fool?'

Aghast, the others shouted at him to keep quiet.

'That's enough,' Lala Kanhaiya Lal said, 'You're crossing your limits. You should know better than to talk about the widow of a respected man like this. If you're so well educated, don't you remember the teachings of our *shastras*?' He looked at Pandit. 'Maharaj! Please continue. Don't pay any attention to this young fool's words. Please tell us how to deal with the girl.'

Karam Chand spoke up, 'I request you all to consider what I have to say first. If this girl had been willing to spend the rest of her life quietly as a widow, I wouldn't have any problem letting her be a part of my family. But I've been noticing her bad intentions for a long time. Still, I kept quiet and let her do whatever she wanted. As you sow, so shall you reap, I thought.

'But she was hell-bent on ruining our family's honour and reputation. What do you want me to do in such circumstances? Are such matters worth discussing publicly? I have always been patient. Now tell me, what should I have done? Should I have tied her up to stop her from going astray? You all saw how she finally left in disgrace.'

'Yes, he's right,' voices echoed around him. 'He did more for her than people do for their own children.'

Pandit thought for a while. 'So, what should be done now?'

Baba Radha Singh adjusted his turban, pushing it slightly up his forehead, and spoke up. 'Those who disgrace their religion lose everything. What can we do about someone who has severed ties from a house of plenty? Let her suffer for her deeds and stay in whatever condition she is in.'

'Yes! Baba ji is right. He has spoken the truth,' everyone chimed.

'I think this girl should be left to her fate. There's nothing to be done for her. What do you say Karam Chand?'

Karam Chand joined his hands together, barely able to keep the excitement from his voice. 'Maharaj, you are wise and learned. I will do whatever you suggest. That girl will never step foot inside my house again. Isn't it said that it's impossible to mend a broken heart or a crushed flower?'

Everyone agreed. Applauding Pandit's wisdom and Karam Chand's intelligence, the men slowly trickled out. With a final '*Hari Om*', Pandit also made a move to leave.

Karam Chand handed him a few silver coins and said, 'Maharaj, please keep your hand of blessing upon us.'

While his coin-filled hand searched for his pocket, Pandit placed his other hand on Karam Chand's shoulder. 'Of course, of course. If I remember correctly, I told you to do something.'

'Yes, Pandit ji, I met Khwaja Sahib that day. He didn't agree at first, but when he remembered your pleas, he finally did.'

'That's great. And about how much—?'

'I paid him fifty rupees in cash and promised to pay the balance fifty after the case is settled.'

'Good, it's a good deal.'

Pandit gave Karam Chand his blessings, and slowly walked towards his home, tapping his walking stick. God only knows who all he visited along the way and gave counsel to.

8

GURDEI WAS DROWNING IN an ocean of worries when she saw Pandit entering the house. After some small talk, he said, 'My child! I've been wandering all over the town today, just for your sake. I arranged a meeting with the village heads and even talked to people I never wished to speak with. I don't know why these people have lost all their senses, why they can't think and do better.'

'Maharaj, if you don't take pains for someone like me, then who else will?' Gurdei said, bowing respectfully before him.

'I haven't been successful, my child.'

'Why, Maharaj?'

'Karam Chand is not agreeing. He says that you have already signed away your share before the elders and can't take any action against them.'

'What did others in the community say?' Gurdei asked in deep despair.

'What power do they have, my child? They can't force anyone. It's not a government court where you can get anything done in your favour.'

'Then, what am I supposed to do?'

'It's a complex situation. We can't even file a petition in the court; it requires too much money.'

'How much money?'

'At least two or three hundred rupees.'

Gurdei held up the gold bangle she was wearing. 'How much is this worth?'

'One hundred, or one hundred and fifty maybe,' Pandit said, eyeing the bangle greedily.

Gurdei was crestfallen.

'Don't worry, my child. I'll manage the remaining money and file the case.'

Gurdei removed the gold bangle from her wrist and placed it before Pandit's feet. Bowing down before him, she said, 'You are my only hope. Only you can bring my sinking ship to the shore.'

Pandit placed his hand on her head, 'May god bless you, my child. From today onward, I take responsibility for this case and assure you of quick action by god's grace. *Hari Om*. But the case may not be in your favour if you stay in the village.'

'But where can I go? Maybe to my parents' house, but I have no one there…'

'I have a friend in Sialkot. If you want, I can send you to his place.'

'Whatever you think is best, Maharaj.'

Pandit picked up the gold bangle and put it in his bag. 'I'll make all the necessary arrangements. Don't worry about anything. Eat some food and try to get some rest.'

'Why should I worry when you're with me, Maharaj? You're my saviour. How can I ever repay your debt?'

Pandit went downstairs, chanting '*Hari Om*', and a servant brought food for Gurdei. After eating, she lay down on a charpai but could not sleep.

After a while, she heard someone coming upstairs. Pandit entered the room, accompanied by a tall young man. 'My child, I think you should go to Sialkot with my friend today,' he said, gesturing at the young man. 'There will be proper arrangements for your stay there. You won't face any problems.'

'I will never forget your kindness,' Gurdei said, looking at him gratefully.

A few hours later, she was on a train to Sialkot with the tall young man.

9

WITHIN A FEW DAYS of reaching Sialkot, the reality of the situation dawned on Gurdei. Pandit, whom she had considered a messiah and worshipped, was nothing but a snake under human skin. After robbing her of her jewellery, he sold her to a man named Tara Chand. The person who had accompanied her to Sialkot was Pandit's pimp. Gurdei found herself absolutely helpless. She had been trapped in Pandit's web of deceit. She had no choice but to surrender herself to Tara Chand.

Tara Chand was semi-literate and worked as a clerk in a government office for thirty rupees a month. He told Gurdei that he was from a town called Gujranwala. He said he didn't live there because his father was upset with him, but the family owned property worth lakhs.

But a lie can't stay hidden for long. A few months later, Tara Chand's actual situation came to light when a letter from his mother arrived. While he was outside the house, Gurdei managed to have the letter read to her. His mother had written: 'I've had to take up all kinds of manual labour to make ends meet, but you haven't sent me a single paisa since you left home. I've also heard you've kept someone else's wife in your house. It is not right...'

Gurdei was helpless. She had no place either with her in-laws' or her own family. She was illiterate and ignorant and had followed anyone who showed her greener pastures. And now she had lost her honour as well.

Still, she felt lucky to have a roof above her head and enough food to survive. But she did not know that the shadows of misfortune were still following her.

As luck would have it, Tara Chand lost his job in one of the retrenchment drives common in government offices those days. Gurdei, meanwhile, had fallen ill and was confined to her bed.

Tara Chand, once madly in love with Gurdei, was now fed up with her. Deceitful and unreliable, he even became reluctant to buy her medicines. Not a single day went without him fighting with her.

Gurdei felt like she was already dead. The torments of the world, being bound to a useless man, impoverishment – she was watching her sorrows get worse, day by day.

If the present was already so horrible, what would the future hold? She trembled from head to toe at the thought. It seemed like she kept trying to outrun death, but death kept waiting for her at every turn. She clearly understood that Tara Chand was absolutely useless. Where would she carry her bundle of sin, the unborn child in her womb now? How and where would she spend the rest of her life? Her heart, exhausted and broken, had no answer to these questions.

At last, the day she had dreaded came. She caught a fever that did not go away. Close to midnight, she felt she was near death. There was no one with her to give her even a drop of water. Tara Chand had left the house two days ago and was not going to return. Before leaving, he had told her not to expect anything from him. 'I don't own a hospital that I can have you treated. How can I look after you when I'm starving to death myself? I'll find a way to earn enough to live on. I don't want anything to do with this miserable situation anymore.' He had left while she was asleep, taking all the valuables from the house.

Unfortunately, there was no Hindu family near Gurdei's house whom she could ask for help. Somehow, she managed to get up from the bed and dragged herself to the water pitcher. It was empty, like her luck. However, there was some stale water still left in the glass. She put it to her mouth with trembling hands. Some water spilt from the glass, and a few drops went into her mouth. Unable to stand any longer, she fell unconscious.

10

RODU, THE JUGGLER, RETURNED home, carrying a little bit of atta and a few chapattis in a small bag. He had been out all day with his pet monkey, Lachho, performing tricks under the scorching June sun.

Rodu lived alone, with no company except Lachho. A torn and patched robe, two clay bowls, a bag, and a few odds and ends were all he possessed. His parents had died after a severe illness when he was a child, and since he was blind in one eye, nobody had married him.

He was in his sixties now, but Rodu was still naïve. He had no understanding of worldly attachments or love. When he heard of anyone deeply in love, he laughed loudly at their foolishness. All he knew was that a person is born and then dies. But he was devoted to god and revered his gurus. Even though he was born an 'untouchable', he considered himself a pious Hindu.

He slipped the bag from his shoulder and hung it on a peg on the wall. He did not have to tie or untie Lachho. She was his companion in life and shared a deep emotional bond with him. Wiping the sweat from his forehead with his finger, he removed his sodden, patched robe and lay down.

After the cool breeze had dried off his sweat, he got up and poured some water into a cup. He found a piece of jaggery in his bag, crushed it with a stone, and added it to the water. He drank more than half of it and kept the rest in another cup for the waiting monkey. She jumped up to grab her cup, emptied it quickly, and returned to where she sat.

After a while, a pack of growling stray dogs appeared outside his hut. Rodu took out the chapatti pieces from his bag and fed them. Having eaten their dinner, the dogs left. Rodu lay down again.

Though he had to cook dinner soon, he fell asleep the moment he lay down. He changed sides, opened his eyes a little, and fell asleep again. But he got up again a minute later, curled his hand like a pipe and brought it to his ear, trying to hear something in the distance. The voice he had heard sounded clearer now. He leapt up and ran in the direction of the voice. Seeing her master rushing out, the monkey followed him.

He ran through the fields, suddenly stopping near a bush. Bending down, he noticed something red. He moved a little forward. It was an infant wrapped in rags, crying incessantly.

Rodu could not bear the baby's cries and the sorry state she was in. He picked her up without thinking twice and brought her to his hut. It was a pleasant night, but the cool breeze was unbearable for the baby. Her lips were turning blue, and she was going numb.

Rodu was scared. What was he going to do with the baby? Where could he take her? How could he save her? Lachho kept coming up to the baby, trying to touch her. Rodu snarled at her and held the infant close in his lap. *She must be hungry*, he thought. He lay her down, grabbed a cup and ran towards the village to get some milk. He was apprehensive about leaving the baby alone with the monkey. *I've made a mistake. I should have brought her with me. If anybody asked, I could have said she belonged to a relative.*

He felt like returning immediately, but the thought of the baby crying with hunger stopped him. He closed his eyes, joined his hands, thought of Shiv ji and Parvati ji, and continued.

Even though he had been quick, it took him half an hour to return with the milk. His heart was thumping against his chest as he rushed back to his hut, afraid that an innocent life would be lost because of his foolishness.

He was astonished when he got back. The monkey was cradling the baby in her lap like a mother. The rags she had been wrapped in were lying to the side. The baby wasn't crying and had opened her eyes, soaking up the warmth of the monkey's body. Seeing her master enter, Lachho quickly put the baby back in her rags and stepped back in fear.

Rodu took a piece of cotton, dipped it in the cup of milk, and started feeding the infant, one drop at a time. She went to sleep as soon as she was fed. Rodu heaved a sigh of relief.

The night was usual; he cooked three chapattis on a stove made from a few pieces of stone by burning some dried wood. He ate two of the chapattis and gave the third to the monkey. He had to sleep without his blanket because he had put one half under the baby and covered her with the other half. He dozed off, carefully hugging her.

At midnight, when he rolled over, he remembered the baby and got up with a start. He lifted the blanket to check on her, but the baby was not there. Traumatized that a wild animal had taken her away, he turned around to look around the hut. The baby was in the hands of Lachho who was feeding her milk with a cotton swab, just like Rodu had done earlier.

Rodu smiled to himself. *God is great*, he thought. *After snatching the baby from her birth mother, He has handed her over to an animal mother.*

For the first time in his life, a hazy ray of love pierced Rodu's frozen heart. He could feel its gentle warmth.

Time passed by. Rodu, who would earlier make a bet with the sun when going to sleep, now got up several times during the night to check on the child. The baby had grown into a little girl. Rodu named her Sundri. Whenever she woke up at night, he held her in a warm embrace and walked up and down for hours, singing lullabies to make her sleep,

> *'Sadke sadke sadd maayiaan,*
> *Chambe diyaan bootiyaan rabb laayiaan…'*
> (I sacrifice myself for the sweet one,
> The jasmine seedling planted by God…)

In the past, Rodu would laugh when he heard such words, but now he got immense pleasure singing them for Sundri.

The innocent baby, thrown into the jaws of death, had miraculously survived to see the world. After all, nobody can harm someone under the protection of god. He had sent her into the world, giving her the task of melting the stone heart of a man like Rodu. How could she fail in her divine calling?

She was a beautiful child. Her small cat-like eyes, fair skin and silky hair were the work of nature's magic. Perhaps Rodu had predicted this beauty when he named her Sundri.

The old Rodu, who used to manage just enough food for two mouths and then slept comfortably in the cool shadow of trees, now left home early in the morning and returned late in the evening. He needed money to raise Sundri.

Soon, he had saved enough money to buy a small bed and some clothes and toys for her. Earlier, he was content with whatever amount people gave him after his performances. But now, he asked for more after each show for Sundri's sake.

He took her along every day when he went out, melting people's hearts with his pleas for help. '*Bawa*! This little girl's mother died when she was born. Please help her.'

Soon, Sundri turned two. If Rodu was deeply attached to Sundri, Lachho was even more so. She did not let the girl out of her sight for a second. In the company of her monkey mother, Sundri had become a skittish child. She did somersaults like a gymnast and tried to climb the pillars supporting the hut. She wanted to imitate the monkey in every way.

Whenever Rodu saw Sundri playing with other children her age, he was overjoyed to see how much they loved her.

She was blessed with a keen sensibility. She easily imitated the actions she saw and pronounced words the same way she heard them.

Rodu made it a point to bring something for Sundri whenever he returned home in the evening. He had become addicted to this routine. Bringing home a toy or a snack for Sundri would charge his feet with electric swiftness, and a yearning would surge in his heart. He felt happy while feeding Sundri, but he felt even more joy when he reached home, and Sundri came running towards him and clung to his legs, having spotted him from a distance. 'Baba! Give me my gift, give me my gift,' she shouted in excitement while searching Rodu's pockets. When he placed a toy or a packet of sweets in her little hands, she jumped, danced and rushed out impatiently to show her friends. It was a golden period in Rodu's life. Even the wealthiest kings and queens could not have felt such happiness and contentment.

However, while playing with other children, Sundri noticed their mothers. When the children quarrelled with each other, they called their mothers and complained, 'Mama! Look, she's kicking me. Mama! He's not giving me my dice.'

The word 'Mama' did not mean anything to Sundri. Baba Rodu and Lachho, the monkey, were her entire world. But when she saw mothers in the neighbourhood doting on their children, she wanted a mother the same way she wanted a friend's toy.

Once, on a calm and clear moonlit night, old Rodu lay on

a thick rug outside his cottage, holding Sundri and swinging her on his knees. He sang to her as he swayed, not stopping despite the weakness in his legs. At the end of the song, he tickled her, and she burst out laughing. It was their favourite game; the joy of it was like an *amrit* for him.

Suddenly, the voice of a child echoed in the distance, 'Mama…'

Sundri stopped laughing. Holding Rodu's chin with her little hands, she asked, 'Baba! Where is my mama?'

What could the poor old man reply to such an innocent but grave question? He kissed Sundri on the forehead and said, 'My child, your mama has gone.'

She asked again, 'Baba, where is my mama?'

'Your mama has gone far away, my little girl.'

'Far away…?'

'Yes, my child.'

'Baba, my mama gone to the moon?' she asked, pointing to the sky.

'Yes, *beta*, she has gone to the moon.'

'Baba, mama… eagle…?'

'Yes, *puttar*, a big eagle took your mama away.'

'Mama… far away… eagle?'

'Yes, my child, the eagle took your mama far away.'

Sundri fell asleep.

11

Ten years later

PASSION, WHETHER POSITIVE OR negative, can transform an individual. It is like a drop of curd, serving as a starter in a bowl of milk, capable of creating another batch of perfect curd. Conversely, if it resembles a drop of sour *kanji*, it has the potential to curdle the milk, ultimately spoiling it.

Bachan Singh, son of Jeeva Singh from the village of Diwanpur, was a passionate man. It happened when he joined the Khalsa College in Amritsar after passing the tenth standard. And this passion completely changed his life.

Bachan Singh must have been eighteen or nineteen years old. Although he had been breathing the pollution of Amritsar for years, clean village blood still ran in his veins. He was well-built and had a strong charismatic face that had started sprouting hair. His fair skin and sweet words had made him the hero of his school. His love of poetry and his penchant for public speaking helped, too. He was the leader of his school's union and played a key role in student meetings and assemblies. He was equally popular in public gatherings, and his poems were widely praised. It wasn't that they spoke about crucial subjects; rather his poems were very simple. But Bachan Singh's melodious recitation turned even bronze into gold. When his energetic voice resounded at a gathering, the audience was left mesmerized.

Several campaigns and assemblies for village improvement were being organized during those days. They aimed at curbing social evils and useless spending in villages.

One such event was organized at Jallianwala Bagh in Amritsar. Around ten thousand people attended. As soon as the stage secretary announced Bachan Singh's name, a roar of excitement spread among his admirers. As he stepped onto the stage, he met ear-splitting cheers.

The audience listened to his poem with a pin-drop silence. At the end, they applauded wildly and asked him to recite it again.

A crowd gathered around Bachan Singh after the assembly. His heart was filled with tremendous joy. He felt as if he was flying through the air rather than walking on solid ground.

When the group of admirers had thinned, a glowing face with a silky white beard appeared before him. The man was in his late fifties. Dressed in a plain white cotton kurta and pyjama, he looked like an angel.

He held Bachan Singh's hand and respectfully led him away from the others.

'Son,' he said, sitting on a patch of grass, 'your poem has drawn me to you.'

Bachan Singh sat down beside him. 'Thank you, Baba ji, I'm grateful for the trouble you took.'

'I'm not very well educated, so I wanted to understand

the meaning of your poem.' The old man took out a small piece of paper and read from it,

'At your sacred feet, my beloved mother India,
I pledge my devotion. I commit my life to serving you.
Roaming the streets and neighbourhoods of my homeland,
I vow to eradicate all the existing evils.'

The poem Bachan Singh had recited at the assembly was quite long, but the old man had only noted down these lines of the poem.

'Baba ji, the meaning of this poem is very simple.'

The old man looked at him affectionately. 'No, son. It's not that simple, it's actually quite complex. Think about it.'

Bachan Singh was quiet, lost in thought.

'Do you understand the meaning of these words, "I swear at your feet"?' the old man asked.

Bachan Singh finally understood. He looked at the old man again, but his eyes could not bear the radiance on the old man's face, and he looked down. He was speechless.

The old man put his hand on Bachan Singh's shoulder. 'Young man, one shouldn't swear falsely. It's a sin.'

Bachan Singh's eyes remained downcast, counting specks of dirt on the ground.

'Son, dedicating your life to service doesn't just mean getting people's applause. If you are passionate about something, you should actually do it instead of just boasting.'

The old man's words opened Bachan Singh's eyes. It was

difficult to understand the significance of those lines. Until then, he had believed that public service meant creating a surge of emotions in the minds of his audience with his words, winning their utmost admiration and basking in that joy. But that day, for the first time, he realized what he had been doing was illusory. He had been hiding his true identity under the mask of goodness. There was a different and superior form of life out there – real life, and he hadn't even realized it until that day.

When Bachan Singh asked the old man, he told him his name was Didar Singh, but he was known as Giani ji. He had come to Amritsar for work and was staying there for a few months.

Bachan Singh's life transformed after that encounter. He began meeting Giani Didar Singh daily. Just a few months in his company brought a phenomenal change in Bachan Singh. He still wrote poetry, but not for the world, only for himself. He never forgot the words Giani ji had repeated, 'I swear at your feet…'

12

BACHAN SINGH HAD NOT intended to go home during the summer vacation. He wanted to tour a few villages to put the ideas of his poems to practise. But when he received a letter informing him about his father's illness, he rushed home immediately.

Jeeva Singh was furious when he saw his son. Bachan Singh, who used to dress sharply in expensive suits, ties and shoes, was now wearing a khadi kurta-pyjama and an ordinary pair of slippers. The sick man wanted to set Bachan Singh straight, but what could he do? Jeeva Singh only had one son, and he didn't want to argue with him. Who knew if the young man might leave the house in a fit of rage and never return?

Finally, it was decided that Bachan Singh would stop his studies and get trained to manage the family business instead.

Bachan Singh was obsessed with the idea of public service, but he could not afford to upset his parents. With a heavy heart, he did as they wished.

One day, on the way to the farmlands to supervise work, he passed the gurdwara and noticed that the main gate was locked. *Why is the gurdwara of such a prominent village of Sikhs in such a state,* he thought. He asked a little boy standing nearby, 'Doesn't this gurdwara have a *Granthi*?'

'He's sitting up there', the little boy said, pointing to an open window on the second floor of the Gurdwara.

Bachan Singh was astonished. He felt the same annoyance one experiences when stray animals tear through your crops while the caretaker stands idly in the field.

'Do you mean Bhai ji performs the Guru Granth Sahib's *parkash* upstairs?'

The little boy did not understand. 'What? *Parsad*? *Karah parsad*? That's only available on Gurpurab.'

Bachan Singh called out a couple of times to the *Granthi*, who stuck his head out of the window. Seeing Jeeva Singh's son standing at the main gate, he rushed downstairs and bowed his head with joined hands. '*Waheguru ji ka Khalsa, Waheguru ji ki Fateh*. I'm so grateful for your kind visit, Sardar ji. You've graced this poor man's hut with the divine touch of your feet. Please, come inside.'

Bachan Singh was keen to talk to the *Granthi*. But he was upset at how the man was describing the gurdwara. He almost turned around to leave but then, changing his mind, followed the *Granthi* upstairs.

Bhai Dasondha Singh was about six and a quarter feet tall. It seemed food only contributed to his skeletal frame instead of adding flesh to his body. His cheeks were so sunken that two small balls could fit in without anyone noticing. It seemed that if his stomach was pressed even slightly, it would rub against his spine. His lower jaw was like a gurdwara without devotees – empty, devoid of teeth. The upper jaw only had four teeth, which protruded from his mouth.

His wiry legs would make anyone question what was supporting the man's tall frame. His navel had popped out a thumb's length, and the flesh on his belly looked like a piece of cloth wrapped over an empty deep dish. His ears were drooping, and the thick beads piercing his lobes had stretched the holes wide enough to allow a carrot to pass through them. When it came to Bhai Dasondha Singh's feet, it seemed as if god, like a baniya, had gotten confused about numbers while measuring their size.

The pillow on the *Granthi*'s bed had become a confectioner's rug, absorbing all the oil from his hair. He hurriedly threw it under the bed and attempted to cover the torn floor mat by folding it over. Moving his upper lip to cover his protruding teeth, he said,

'Please sit, Sardar ji, and make yourself at home. You hardly ever visit this place. Today, god has come to an ant's house.'

'By your grace,' Bachan Singh said, looking around the room. 'Where is the *parkash* of the Guru Granth Sahib performed?'

'What can I say, Sardar ji? Hardly anyone comes here,' the *Granthi* said. He thought momentarily and added, 'It's performed downstairs, but I'm not feeling very well today, so I had to skip it.'

Bachan Singh was not a child. Their short conversation was enough for him to understand what was going on. Still, to test the man, he said, 'Let's go downstairs. Please open the door and perform Guru Granth Sahib's *parkash*. I haven't had the chance to pray since I've returned home.'

Bhai Dasondha Singh had no choice but to go downstairs. After searching for more than five minutes, he found the key to the door. But he could not open the lock.

'Are you using the right key?' Bachan Singh asked sternly.

'Wait, it might've been changed.' The *Granthi* mumbled an excuse and started back up the stairs. He quickly doused the rusted key in oil from the lamp and returned.

As soon as the door opened, the *Granthi* said, 'Ah, see, I was wondering why it wasn't opening. The key was lying in another cupboard. I must have brought the wrong one in a hurry.'

When they entered the room and looked at its condition, the two of them began to shake – Bachan Singh out of anger and Bhai Dasondha Singh out of shame.

Aghast, Bachan Singh bombarded the *Granthi* with a flurry of warnings and admonishments. Then he stormed out and proceeded towards his farms.

13

'HELLO, BHAI JI! HOW are you? I hope you're flying high these days', Pala Singh said warmly to Bhai Dasondha Singh, who was sweeping the courtyard.

The *Granthi* set the broom upright in a corner and wiped his dusty hands on his kurta.

'Welcome, welcome! I don't know what to say, Maharaj, Sardar Jeeva Singh's son has made our lives so chaotic. Ever since he's come to the village, he's been getting on our nerves. We poor folks can't even say anything. The high and mighty are always right after all.'

Pala Singh was a notorious goon in the village. He had leased out the bits of land that his family owned as soon as his parents had died. His gang worshipped him like a guru and the entire village feared him. He showed up with his men whenever there was a fight or trouble in the village.

It's not that he didn't share his earnings with his followers. He went on a round, stealing from others, once or twice a month, and later made sure to stop at the gurdwara. That is why he had such a cordial relationship with Bhai Dasondha Singh. Whenever he hit the jackpot, he gave a hefty chunk to the gurdwara, and a *langar* with booze was arranged from his donations.

Pala Singh had been away on one of these rounds and had returned to the village with a big bounty after several days.

He had long disliked Jeeva Singh because he refused to be cowed down by Pala Singh and had even reported his crimes to the police a couple of times. He always felt threatened by Jeeva Singh, and his hatred had extended to Bachan Singh.

'How dare that little boy talk to you disrespectfully? Tell me how he's troubling you.'

'Don't ask, Maharaj. He's part of this new educated generation that keeps trying to make their own stupid rules. He's asked me to get up early every day and perform the *parkash* of the Guru Granth Sahib, clean the gurdwara compound every morning and evening, and do *Rehras paath* every evening.'

Pala Singh furrowed his brow.

'He's gone mad. He seems to think he's in Amritsar. Who can neglect their farms and come to the gurdwara every day? It's enough if people sit for some time on a special occasion like *Sangrand* or *Masya*. But, Bhai ji, why are you so afraid of him? Are you answerable to him or Jeeva Singh?'

Encouraged by the words in his favour, the *Granthi* continued, 'May God bless your children! You're absolutely right. But who can make these people understand? People like me are always dependent upon others. What can we do? We also have to manage our livelihood. If we dare speak a word against their instructions, they warn us not to argue. So we keep quiet and accept everything. And why should we make any unnecessary trouble? Nobody bothers to offer even a chapatti to anyone else here. It's only because of generous people like you, or maybe if someone is involved in a court case or something when people want to do *paath* and offer us some money. Otherwise, no one cares to come here. So why should we spoil our sleep by getting up early in the morning?'

'That's why everyone can put a saddle on your back, Bhai ji. Is this any way to make ends meet? Don't listen to his demands or threats. Just say no. Let's see what harm he can do to you. No one can dare ask you for an explanation if I'm around.'

Bhai ji's barely hidden fervour was now fully charged. 'No, Sardar ji', he burst out enthusiastically. 'Why should I care about him? I was afraid you might blame me for being under his influence. I kept quiet thinking of you, otherwise I'd have told him off right then and there. Sardar ji, you know I need to sleep deeply after some opium. And early morning is the best time for sleep. Oh, and I didn't even tell you the other job he's bent on getting me to do.'

'What's that?'

'He tells me, "Bhai ji, you're idle throughout the day. Instead of wasting time lying in bed for hours, you should teach the village children; you should educate them."'

Pala Singh bit his lip with rage.

'No! There's no need to educate anyone. He should look at himself first. What has he achieved after studying for twelve years? He used to be such a nice boy and handsome, too. And now, having learned a few zigzagged letters, he's completely lost his mind. Look at his clothes. He's the son of Jatts, but he dresses like a homeless man. How did you respond?'

'I'm not under any obligation to him. I told him plainly that I can't take on the hassle of educating every boy and girl in the village. And, Sardar ji, I need my daily dose of opium at noon, and then I've got to get enough rest. I don't have time for all this nonsense.'

'Bhai ji, enjoying your daily dose all alone? Dhiyan Singh and Narain Singh have been telling me since morning to see you for some *charnamrit*.'

'Maharaj, I've been so worried about this boy. I've been dry for days now.'

'Don't start your complaints again now, Bhai ji. I'm telling you, don't be scared of this boy. I'll handle him. Enjoy your dose of *ragda* today; I'd like to see him try and boss you around.'

'Let's make up for these lost days then. Why don't you join us?'

'I will!'

'Please try your best to come before sunset. And don't forget to bring your friends.'

'They're the ones who've been insisting. We'll be there.'

'I'm so happy to hear that.'

'*Waheguru ji ki fateh*,' Pala Singh said and left.

Bhai Dasondha Singh threw down the broom and started preparations for the evening. He'd had a couple of pinches of opium in the morning, but there was hardly any pleasure in savouring it all alone. Sitting with friends and consuming generous amounts was much more joyous than small, lonely pinches.

14

IT WAS AROUND 3 P.M. Bhai Dasondha Singh and the other men had gathered in the hall on the first floor of the gurdwara. Sitting in a corner, Bhai ji was tenderly cleaning the grinding bowl. He hadn't gotten the chance to clean it for several days out of fear of Bachan Singh.

Pala Singh took a piece of jaggery from his pocket and kept it aside. 'Bhai ji, pick up the pace.'

Still wiping the bowl with a rag, Bhai ji said, 'All right, Maharaj, you mix the jaggery in this bowl, and I'll rush to the market to get what we need for the *shardai*.'

A young man got up and started mixing the jaggery. Another started cleaning the opium. The *Granthi* wiped his wet hands on his kurta and was about to leave for the market when Pala Singh pulled out a four-anna coin from his pocket and gave it to Bhai ji. 'Ask him to make it with extra flavour – two annas for the *shardai* and two for the almonds.'

Gopal Singh opened a small dirty pouch. 'Bhai ji, don't bother with the almonds,' he said, pouring nearly a kilo of almonds.

'All right, just buy the *shardai* with all of it,' Pala Singh said.

The *Granthi* reached the market quickly, thinking that the Jatts had lost their minds. He bought the *shardai* for two annas and slipped the remaining two into his pocket.

When he returned, the men were cracking open the raw almond shells. 'Bhai ji, you took so long. Come on, give me the stuff,' Deva Singh said, extending his hand.

The *Granthi* pulled the packet out so hurriedly that it opened inside his pocket. Some of the stuff spilt on the floor. Everyone burst out laughing. He still seemed high since the morning.

Embarrassed, he emptied the stuff from his pocket into the grinding bowl. 'See these baniyas! They're taught to run their shops from birth, but still, they don't know how to pack anything properly.'

The opium was cleaned and put into the bowl. The men sat in a circle and started grinding one by one. After about an hour, when the opium had become a fine powder, Lakha Singh said, 'Can you stop grinding, or do you want to spend the whole night doing it?'

The *Granthi* was cleaning the glasses in a corner. He wiped off the oil residue from a bowl with his kurta. 'Not yet, Maharaj, mash it up a little more. There's a famous saying,

"Sukha ghottan sain mein, jetaa karo vilamb,

Tetaa hi bahu gun kare, kahe Shiv Shambhu aap."'

(The more you mash the stuff; the more potent its effect. This is what Lord *Shiva Shambhu* says.)

A Nirmala sadhu was among the men gathered in the gurdwara. He was sitting near them, reading a holy book.

Distracted by the *Granthi*, he looked up. 'Bhai ji, you seem to be a poet, but your words don't rhyme properly.'

Keen to impress the sadhu, the *Granthi* said, 'Maharaj, this poem is based on a verse called "sirkhandi-chhand". Many renowned poets followed this verse while writing their poems. One of them wrote,

"Mukh par gang suhai, vishav nath kailash pat.
Jou bhaje sukh paye, man chit seti dhiyan dhar".'

No one could understand what he recited, and the sadhu couldn't control his laughter. 'Bhai ji, this is called a *sortha*. And it looks like this poem is your own creation. "*Mukh par gang suhai...*" Amazing! What a metaphor! Did the Ganga originate from Shiv ji's mouth or head?'

Under the influence of opium, the *Granthi* had forgotten that an actual wise man was sitting with the group of idiots. He scratched the corn on his foot with his fingernail and continued defending himself with more foolish explanations.

The sadhu laughed loudly again. 'All right, Bhai ji,' he finally said, 'you really are a learned person.' The other men applauded.

The two of them had argued for half an hour by this point. 'Bhai ji, can I stop grinding now?' Piara Singh asked, collecting the residue from the sides of the pestle with his finger.

'Enough, Maharaj, enough' the *Granthi* said. He pulled his muffler from a nail on the wall, moved a little forward and sat down. A cracking sound came from his knees as he sat as if someone had ignited a fire. Pala Singh picked up the jaggery. 'Bhai ji, please make two drinks – one for us veterans, and the other for the newbies.' He pointed to his left. 'This young man is the son-in-law of Ganda Singh. He has come to his in-laws' house for the first time. Don't give him too much, or he'll start avoiding us. Vasava Singh and Mann Singh are also new to this.'

'All right,' Bhai ji said, resuming his preparation. Soon, everything was ready.

Partap Singh, the son-in-law of Ganda Singh, lived in the city but was not educated, even though he looked nothing less than a graduate in his necktie and sharp collar. Unsure of himself and his first tryst with opium, he prayed that everything would go well.

When he saw his turn coming, Partap Singh tapped the *Granthi*'s back and whispered, 'Bhai ji, please make *swaya gaffa* (moderate quantity) for me.'

The *Granthi* was unfamiliar with the term. Without even turning back and looking at Partap Singh, he assumed the man was asking for a strong drink. Servers of opium usually get annoyed with such requests. Those who boast of handling large quantities are usually served doses strong enough to break their pride forever.

This is what the *Granthi* did with Partap Singh. Instead of filling his glass from the pot with the weak mixture, he reached for the stronger one. He even scraped the bottom of the pot to get the more concentrated mixture, making the drink even more potent.

Despite Partap Singh's repeated requests to 'make a light drink; make a smaller one,' the *Granthi* poured him a full glass. Partap Singh sipped at it hesitatingly, leaving about a fourth of the drink in his glass.

The men started chatting. Ujgar Singh rubbed his hand over his face. 'Wow! It feels great! I feel like I shouldn't even say anything. What an aroma, like ripened flowers.'

Pursing his lips and squeezing his eyelids shut, Inder Singh replied, 'What did you say? Flowers bloom, not ripen. It's fruits that ripen.'

Bhan Singh opened his eyes wide. 'What happened, Pala Singh, getting a kick with just the first glass? You're a longtime sinner, but you've started squinting so soon!'

Pala Singh swallowed his saliva with difficulty. 'What do you mean?' Rubbing his lips and cheeks vigorously with his fingers, he continued, 'Bhan Singh! I never get a kick so easily. I swear by my guru, even if I have the entire batch, I'd be fine. It's just my nature; I never get high.'

After a pause, he continued, 'Bhan Singh! You're asking about my condition, but I notice your eyes are closing.'

'What did you say?' Bhan Singh asked, jerking himself into alertness. 'No, no, I'm not feeling anything.'

'Not feeling anything! Your eyes are saying it all!'

'If you don't believe me, ask me anything, and you'll get a straight answer.'

'Okay,' Pala Singh said, thinking. 'What happened with the Kamokianwala court case?'

Pala Singh waited for an answer, but when he looked

at Bhan Singh, he found him staring at the ceiling. Excited about his victory, he was about to say something but forgot everything the next moment. He tried to concentrate but could not remember what they were discussing. He focused more intently but had even forgotten whom he was talking to. At last, after great effort, he recalled the subject of their conversation as if he had found a lost treasure. Afraid of forgetting again, he said hurriedly, 'Yes! Bhan Singh, tell me about the outcome of the Kamokianwala court case.'

Bhan Singh's concentration was broken, but he couldn't understand what Pala Singh was talking about. 'What did you say?'

Pala Singh widened his eyes. 'What? I didn't say anything.' He thought for a while. 'Oh yes, I was saying don't put that brown bull to work tomorrow. The poor animal was working the whole night at the well.'

Bhan Singh wet his lips with this tongue. 'Leave it, you were saying… you were saying…' Forgetting his own words, he said, 'Yes… I'd met him… but he charged me two rupees… and went away.' He laughed.

Pala Singh put his hand on his face. 'Bhan Singh, it's strange, I've never been so, so…'

As he talked, he realized he was hungry. The jaggery left after making their drinks had already been eaten. 'Bhai ji, go and get something to eat.'

The *Granthi* was swaying from side to side. Without saying a word, he took one rupee and went out. While turning towards the market, he forgot what he had gone out for.

But he recovered his memory soon and reached the grocery shop. He bought fifty paisa worth of *reori* and returned to the gurdwara, concentrating intently.

The entire group of men was lying flat. One stared at the ceiling in deep concentration, one laughed loudly, and another leaned forward like he meant to call someone but had frozen in that position like a statue.

The men who were asleep stayed that way, but for the ones awake, the *reoris* were like a ghost's meal. Pala Singh gave the *Granthi* one more rupee to get more reories. He could have refused, but the thought of earning another half-rupee was too tempting, and he couldn't eat even a single *reori*. He started for the market again.

He was trying his best to stay focused on the purpose of his visit so he wouldn't get distracted and end up somewhere else. He was like a man who did not know how to swim, clutching onto a raft desperately so he wouldn't drown.

He was not sure where he had kept his muffler. He even forgot that the fresh packet of *reoris*, which he had just bought, was tied to the muffler. He started looking everywhere for the packet.

When the *Granthi* didn't return for quite some time, Pala Singh remembered the *reoris*. He rushed to the market to look for Bhai Dasondha Singh but did not return either.

The sadhu had enough experience when it came to opium. After about an hour, when the intoxication started to subside, he too remembered his companions who had not returned with *reoris*. He immediately got up and went to look for them. Dusk had fallen; it was time to turn on the lights.

The sadhu reached the market and looked for the two men everywhere but couldn't find them. He started returning to the gurdwara. On his way, he saw a large mud hole where the water from a nearby well had accumulated. Pala Singh was lying in it face down. Several men were shaking him, but he kept repeating the same thing.

'I'm on fire', he shouted, 'my clothes too! My belly has cooled down with water, but my back is still burning. Pour a bucket full of water on it! I'm dying!'

The sadhu watched silently and returned to the gurdwara, but the *Granthi* was still not there. He was about to lie down when his foot touched something under the bed. When he looked, he found Bhai Dasondha Singh hiding under there, still clinching the rupee coin tightly in his fist.

The sadhu tried to pull him out by shaking him, but the *Granthi* kept shrinking further, 'Catch hold of Bachan Singh, Pala Singh! You assured me…' He giggled. 'Hurry up, look… he's squeezing my neck. He's going to…,' he swallowed with great difficulty, 'kill me.'

'Someone help', he continued rambling, 'my mouth is filling with sand. It's getting so dry, take this sand out of my mouth.'

Everyone else was lying flat on the ground. Who would listen to the *Granthi*'s wailing?

With night falling, the sadhu was worried about the figures stretched on the ground. He started shaking them one by one. Everyone got up and walked away, dangling their arms, but Partap Singh did not wake up despite endless attempts. The sadhu got frightened. He considered gathering his things and running away. But thinking it difficult to leave in his state, he lay back in bed.

The next day, when the sun rose high, the sadhu got up from his bed and stretched his body, followed by a few yawns. He looked all around but couldn't find the *Granthi*. He got afraid. He recalled the events of the previous night and how the *Granthi* had been hiding beneath his bed, but now he was nowhere to be seen. The other young man, lying face down, was also not there.

The sadhu slipped away from the gurdwara in a panic. He had hardly walked half a kilometre when he saw Bachan Singh coming from the opposite direction carrying Bhai Dasondha Singh on his shoulder. But he kept moving, avoiding Bachan Singh's eyes.

15

THERE WAS AN UPROAR in the village. Every household was talking about the opium episode. Most families had managed to cover up for their relatives who had been a part of it, but Ganda Singh's family was still greatly disturbed. Their son-in-law had visited them for the first time, and now the poor man was in such a bad state that he hadn't been able to close his eyes once throughout the night. Bachan Singh had carried the unconscious man to their house. He told them when he went to the gurdwara, the *Granthi* was nowhere to be seen, but a sadhu was sleeping on the bed, and Partap Singh was lying unconscious on the floor.

Ganda Singh's family tried their best to bring the boy back to his senses. They put drops of oil in his ears and massaged his head. They stuffed mango pickle in his mouth, but it did not pass through his lips. They tried to make him drink a mixture of milk and ghee, but it dripped out of his mouth.

His condition gradually began to worsen. His eyes turned glassy, his face turned blue, and his body turned stiff like a log. Everyone panicked. The next morning, a doctor was called from a nearby government hospital. After examining him, the doctor declared that the man had been poisoned.

He was taken to the hospital.

Pala Singh and his companions were panicking as well. After all, a guilty man gets killed by his own conscience. Pala Singh was worried that the police would find out about his involvement in the incident. His name was in the criminal records a few years ago, and he had worked very hard to win the favour of the authorities. He had greased enough palms to get his name cleared from the records, but Partap Singh's condition scared him.

So, he hatched a plot to kill two birds with a single stone. Even before the police could swing into action, he filed a report stating that Jeeva Singh's son, Bachan Singh, had poisoned Ganda Singh's son-in-law by giving him contaminated opium.

The police rushed to Bachan Singh's house. Deputing a constable to keep guard, the officer then went to Ganda Singh's house.

As the constable searched Bachan Singh's house, the officer went to the gurdwara to investigate, accompanied by a task force. When they entered Bhai Dasondha Singh's room, they found Bachan Singh massaging the *Granthi*'s head with oil. He was sitting in front of Bachan Singh, rocking from side to side. Despite his distaste for the *Granthi*'s vices, Bachan Singh's conscience did not allow him to ignore a man in distress, and he had tried to bring him back to consciousness by massaging his head.

The police took both of them into custody and started searching the room. They found what they were looking for without much effort. A cotton rag, used as a filter while cleaning the raw opium, was lying in a corner. The *Granthi* had thrown it aside hurriedly without washing it or disposing of the residue.

A doctor was called in. When he crushed the dry residue to test it for contamination, he found two mangled bronze coins, ground so severely that they got reduced to half their original size.

The doctor concluded that Partap Singh had been made to drink the residue of those coins blended in the process of preparing the opium drink. Bachan Singh and the *Granthi* were handcuffed.

Pala Singh and his men were waiting nearby. They were amazed at the sight of coins emerging from the opium residue. They did not understand how they had gotten into the drink but were glad that Bachan Singh had so easily fallen into the police's net. And he had been caught at the scene of the crime. Partap Singh's in-laws had also recorded in their statement that Bachan Singh had brought the boy home around 9 p.m. Pala Singh decided to bribe the police.

Both suspects were charge-sheeted, and a case was filed in court. Jeeva Singh was suffering from a high fever, but a lawyer was hired on his behalf.

Pala Singh's evidence was recorded as, 'On the day of the incident, I was at my house. At 5 p.m., when I went to the Gurdwara, Bachan Singh and Partap Singh were grinding opium. Bhai ji was busy in meditation. After sitting there for some time, I returned home. At around 9 p.m., I saw Bachan

Singh walking down the street. He was carrying Partap Singh on his back to drop him at his in-laws' house. I called him several times, but he didn't respond.'

Next, a few members of Pala Singh's gang recorded their statements, which were almost the same as each other.

The statements of the accused were also recorded; the *Granthi* said what he had been taught, 'Bachan Singh had instructed me to grind the opium mixture. He also gave me four anna coins to buy *shardai* from the market. I spent two annas to buy—,' saying this the *Granthi* paused.

The Magistrate, an Anglo-Indian, asked the government lawyer to explain some of the words he was using.

The *Granthi* continued with his statement. 'My Lord! I bought *shardai* for two annas. You can make me swear on anything.'

Bachan Singh's lawyer was a professional.

'Where did you buy the *shardai*?' he asked.

'From Lala Devi Dyal's shop.'

'How much did you pay him?'

'Four annas.'

'And how much did he return to you?'

'Two annas.'

'All right, how many coins did he give you?'

Pala Singh discreetly showed him two fingers, trying to give him the connecting pieces for their story, but the *Granthi* was not that smart. 'Eight paisa', he said.

'What did you do with that money?' The lawyer asked.

'I kept it in the pocket of my kurta.'

'And what about the packet of *shardai*?'

'That was in the same pocket, too.'

'Where did you put the money when you returned to the gurdwara?'

Something suddenly struck the *Granthi*. 'Later, I found six coins in my pocket instead of eight. Maybe two coins fell into the grinding bowl... no, I mean,' he paused to think again, 'those two coins might have fallen out somewhere else.'

'And what about the coins found in the opium residue?'

The *Granthi*'s legs started trembling, and his bare knees knocked against each other. He could sense the picture getting clearer, and he fumbled even more.

'You won't be harmed if you speak the truth,' the lawyer continued. 'Otherwise, you'll be in jail for life.'

The *Granthi*'s few remaining gods also vanished into thin air. He joined his hands together. 'Sir, I'll tell you the truth. Those coins accidentally fell off my pocket into the grinding vessel and got mixed in with the *shardai*. I only got to know about it later.'

Pala Singh and his buddies were petrified. The oars of their boat were in the hands of a hopeless rower, and they could drown at any moment.

The lawyer patted the *Granthi*'s back. 'Well done! I'm glad to hear you speak the truth. Real Sikhs and *Granthi*s of your stature never lie.' The lawyer's pat transformed Bhai Dasondha Singh. He told the whole court the truth and stated that Bachan Singh didn't have a hand in the incident.

Bachan Singh's statement was recorded next. He said, 'I was at the revenue office from 7 a.m. My father had sent me there to settle a land dispute. At around 8 p.m., when I entered the village, I thought about meeting the *Granthi* to discuss a plan to open a school for the village children.

'I went to his room on the first floor of the gurdwara, but he wasn't there. I saw a Nirmala sadhu lying on the bed and Partap Singh on the floor. I tried to wake them up, but they didn't stir. When I saw the utensils and hand grinder next to them, I realized they had consumed opium. I panicked upon seeing Partap Singh's condition. He's the son-in-law of a family in this village and deserved looking after, so I lifted him on my back and took him to his in-laws' house.

'The next morning, when I was going to the fields, someone told me that a Sikh was lying unconscious on the river bank. I rushed there and found Bhai ji. I lifted him and brought him back to the gurdwara. I did my best to bring him back to consciousness by massaging his head. Bhai ji told me, "I don't know when I hid under the bed under the effect of opium. Later in the evening, when I felt like defecating, I dragged myself out of the village to a mango grove nearby. After relieving myself, I turned but lost my way and reached the river instead. I fell unconscious there."'

After that, Partap Singh's statement had to be recorded. He was still in the hospital and was hardly in a condition to speak. Although he tried to repeat the lies taught to him beforehand, he could not withstand the lawyer's scrutiny.

The course of the lawsuit was now reversed. Pala Singh, five of his accomplices and the *Granthi* were arrested as per the court's orders. After a few more witnesses and hearings, the court issued its verdict, 'Bachan Singh is absolved of all charges. Bhai Dasondha Singh is sentenced to one-year imprisonment for putting a life in danger due to sheer ignorance. Pala Singh is sentenced to rigorous imprisonment for two years for filing a false report under Section 177 of the Indian Penal Code. The remaining five are sentenced to imprisonment for six months each for presenting false testimony.'

16

THOUGH PALA SINGH, HIS accomplices and Bhai Dasondha Singh had reaped the fruits of their own misdeeds, they blamed Bachan Singh for their sentencing. Pala Singh's associates desperately awaited his release to settle the score. They spread the word in the village that Bachan Singh had begun the hostility with Pala Singh by mixing coins in their opium drink and had trapped them all by manipulating Bhai Dasondha Singh's evidence.

Bachan Singh, meanwhile, was convinced that the root cause for the deplorable condition in the village was a lack of education. It was the only explanation for why people were ruining their futures and those of their families by having opium sessions at a holy place like a gurdwara.

While leaving Amritsar, Bachan Singh had sought a promise from Giani Didar Singh to visit his village. He sent a message to the old saint, who agreed to come immediately.

Giani Didar Singh lived in Sialkot, where his two sons ran a small business. Having dedicated much of his life to performing the duties of a family man, he had decided a while ago to spend the rest of his time serving man. His sons had arranged to send him ten rupees monthly, no matter where he was. In addition, he had his personal savings.

Bachan Singh was incredibly thankful for Giani ji's arrival. When he described the condition of his village and the surrounding areas, the pain in his words brought tears to Giani ji's eyes. Even as he commiserated with Bachan Singh, he noticed a remarkable change in his personality and marvelled at how honest and courageous the young man had become.

Finally, when Bachan Singh showed him the pathetic condition of the gurdwara, Giani ji couldn't bear it any more and decided he would live in Diwanpur for a while.

Giani ji was a devout religious man, simple and soft-spoken. He woke up early, bathed, recited *paath,* and then performed the Guru Granth Sahib's *parkash* at the gurdwara. His arrival proved advantageous to the farmers in the village as well because they woke up early every morning when they heard the squeaking sound of the *bhauni* when Giani ji drew water from the well for his bath, collected their yokes and went to their fields.

Giani ji's presence in the village influenced the farmers' wives too. On their way to the fields to gather spinach or to deliver food to their husbands, they stopped at the gurdwara to pay obeisance and offered a handful of grains, cotton flower buds, or a couple of corn cobs.

Over time, when the farmers were on their way to the fields or returning from them, they placed their tools along the gurdwara wall, pushed the cattle ahead, and paid obeisance at the gurdwara, whether from outside or inside.

Giani ji took on the responsibility of educating the village children with the relentless assistance of Bachan Singh. A carpenter was engaged to make ten to fifteen *takhti*s for the students to write on. A bundle of reeds was used to make *kalams*, a potter was hired to make inkpots, and the writing tools were distributed among the children. Getting them to show interest in classes was difficult since they weren't used to sitting in one place for hours. But Giani ji persisted, gently and lovingly.

Before he could finish working with one student, another would shout, 'Giani ji! Mangu has broken my *kalam*.' By the time he would sharpen a new one for him, another would complain, 'Giani ji! Banta is mimicking me.' Then two girls, sitting on the other side of the room, would start quarrelling, and Giani ji would have to deal with them.

Giani ji laboured for nearly two months to teach the mischievous children, but he managed only to make them sit in the classroom. The unruly kids giggled at Giani ji's long snow-white beard flowing freely over his chest. If he left the room even for a moment, the girls removed their scarves from their heads, folded them into balls, and threw them at each other using their *takhti*s. They tied their pigtails together and clapped and danced. But Giani ji was dedicated to the cause and was confident of succeeding.

One day, Giani ji and Bachan Singh were deep in discussion in the classroom while the boys and girls read on a rug in front. They were talking about *sewa*. '*Sewa*, in fact, is an extremely difficult practice,' Giani ji said. 'Very often, the tasks people perform in the name of *sewa* are just pretensions.'

Every word coming out of Giani ji's mouth was making a deep impact on Bachan Singh. He was about to ask a question when his attention was diverted to the classroom's open door. A girl was standing outside. She must have been anywhere between twelve and fourteen years old. She was carrying a straw basket filled with garbage on her head and was finding it difficult to balance its weight. When her neck got tired, she moved the basket to her arms and then back again. Even though she was shrouded in poverty, her moon-like face gleamed bright.

Bachan Singh noticed that some students sitting near the door were making fun of the girl. They exchanged glances and glared at her scornfully. One of the girls chucked sugarcane peels at her, another pulled straws from her basket and threw them at her, and yet another spat at her while passing by.

But the girl was oblivious to the bullying, concentrating on their books, *takhtis*, and handwriting instead. When she hoisted the basket up with her hands, yet again to her head, the padded ring she rested it on fell to the ground. The classroom burst into laughter, and the poor, embarrassed girl could not bear to stay any longer and ran off.

When Giani ji admonished the girls, they became quiet and hid their faces behind their *takhtis*. Bachan Singh told Giani ji how he saw them taunting the poor girl. Giani ji was furious. 'Pay attention!' he said loudly, 'don't create a nuisance in the class.' He turned to Bachan Singh. 'They are a pain in the neck. Despite all my efforts, they refuse to mend their ways…'

Bachan Singh interrupted him. 'Giani ji, it is out of the kindness of your heart that you're educating them.' He gestured towards the students and continued, 'Otherwise, are these rascals worth teaching? They only know how to handle their livestock.'

Bachan Singh sat and talked about other matters with Giani ji for a while and then left.

17

WHILE RETURNING HOME ONE evening, Rodu realized he had not brought a gift for Sundri in the last several days. He unfolded his turban and found some coins. Then he searched his robe and bag for money. Sitting by the road, he counted all the change, which came to three annas. He thought for a while about what he could buy with that money. Finally, he remembered that Sundri had been clamouring for a harp. He went to a nearby shop and bought one for two-and-a-half annas. With the rest of the money, he bought some sweets.

When he reached home, he left the monkey at the door and entered the house, calling 'Sundro! Sundro!' But today, unlike other days, Sundri wasn't waiting eagerly for him.

He rushed out and looked for her everywhere, shouting out her name, but to no avail. He became furious, and it was difficult to gauge how much love and anxiety blended with his fury.

Eventually, he went to the rear of the cottage and found Sundri sitting behind a cot, writing something on the ground with her finger.

Poor Rodu heaved a sigh of relief. When she caught sight of him, Sundri forgot all about writing. She clung to his waist, smiling, and pulled him towards her. 'Look here, Baba... here...' she said, jumping excitedly, as she ran ahead of him as if she had found a treasure.

Rodu's heart filled with love at her innocent joy. He pulled her close and kissed her head. 'My child! What are these strange figures you're drawing?'

'Yes, strange figures.' She touched the letters of the alphabet with her finger. 'Look, Baba, this is Oorah, this is Sassa, and this is... wait, I've forgotten... oh yes, this is Pappa.'

How would poor Rodu know about these strange things called 'Sassa' or 'Pappa'? He laughed out loud. 'Wow, my sweet little scholar! How do you know how to write all this?'

'They were writing like this, Baba!'

'Who?'

'Those girls, who else?'

'Which girls?'

'The girls studying at the gurdwara.'

'But, how do you know they write like this, my little Sundro?'

'I watch them writing every day, Baba. I watched them today also. When I went to throw away the garbage, I saw them writing.'

'So, let them do it; it's none of your concern.'

Sundri swayed like a little child with a pout on her face. 'No, Baba,' she said, with a hint of mischief in her voice, 'I'll also write the way those girls do.'

Rodu laughed ruefully and held her chin. 'See, this great

scholar! Silly girl! Is this reading and writing any of our business?'

Sundri's heart filled with despair. She looked at him with questioning eyes. 'Then whose business is it?'

'My dear child, those girls' families are a different sort. We're poor beggars, and beggars don't study. What do we have to do with such things?'

Sundri turned pale when she heard his words as if she had done something wrong. But, the next moment, quivering like a baby goat, she asked, 'We... we can't... study?'

'*Beta*, you know what they say. If people of lower castes start getting an education, then who will perform all the jobs that we do?'

Sundri refused to accept Rodu's explanation. 'No, Baba', she said, her voice obstinate, 'I'll write. I'll write sitting inside. How will they know? I'll go there pretending to dispose of the garbage, memorise the letters those girls are writing, and then later in the evening...'

'Forget all this nonsense', Rodu interrupted. 'Here, take this.' He handed her the harp and the packet of sweets.

Sundri had finally gotten the harp she had been demanding for weeks. Rodu waited for her to jump with excitement when she saw it, but the girl took the gifts and kept them carelessly in a corner, unopened.

18

BACHAN SINGH MADE IT a point to meet Giani ji regularly. They discussed something new every day, and these conversations had a transformative effect on Bachan Singh; the stream of his life began taking a different course.

Often, Bachan Singh noticed the girl with the broken straw basket on her head or in her arms. She stood for hours near the entrance of the classroom and watched the boys and girls writing.

One day, when he came to the gurdwara in the afternoon, he saw Giani ji preparing to go somewhere after giving instructions to the students.

'Where are you going?' he asked.

'I was waiting for you. My clothes have become dirty, and I need to go to the well to wash them. I thought I'd take you along for company.'

'All right, let's go', Bachan Singh said. When they came out of the classroom, they saw the girl. She had emptied her basket and kept it on the side. She sat facing the wall, scribbling something in the moist soil with her finger. She looked at a torn piece of paper lying beside her and then wrote with her finger. The paper was the first page of a

Punjabi alphabet book with the thirty-five letters printed in bold. The girl had carefully stuck small cloth strips around its edges. She considered it precious as if it were a royal announcement.

Giani ji and Bachan Singh watched her for several minutes, captivated by her beautiful handwriting. While writing the last letter of the alphabet, she looked at the paper and suddenly became aware of the two men standing near her. Frightened, she started to run away, leaving her empty basket behind.

She had hardly run three or four steps when Giani ji called after her, 'Hey, you!'

The girl's first thought was to continue running, but it was as if her legs were not ready to move any further, and she stopped immediately. 'Don't be afraid, my child,' Giani ji continued, 'I won't scold you. Come here and listen to me.'

The girl slowly walked back to them with the bowed head of an accused criminal and stood in front of them. 'Where did you learn to write these letters?' Giani ji asked her gently.

The girl trembled. She knew that he was trying to get her to admit her crime, but she couldn't come up with an answer to Giani ji's question.

He patted her head softly and pulled her slightly close. '*Kaake*! Don't be afraid. I'm not going to harm you. I was so happy to see your beautiful handwriting. Who taught you to write like that?'

The girl felt a sense of relief but was shy. She finally spoke softly, 'I write all by myself.'

Bachan Singh had been watching all this in wonder. 'All by yourself?' he asked, 'Didn't you learn from anyone?'

Both men were thrilled when they heard her say no. 'Can you read these letters?' Giani ji asked.

'Yes.'

'Read them out loud.'

The girl recited all thirty-five letters flawlessly. 'I come here every day and stand near the classroom', she said, 'I hear the students reading the letters out loud.'

Giani ji patted her on the back. 'Well done, my child! You're so intelligent. Wait, I'll bring a book and *takhti* for you. What's your name?'

'Ji, Sundri.'

'Giani ji,' Bachan Singh said, 'I think she is the daughter of *achhoots*, and you are touching her without fear. I don't care about these things, but the people of this village can be very narrow-minded.'

Giani ji went inside and brought back a book, a *takhti*, two *kalams* and an inkpot and handed them to the girl. 'Take these with you and keep studying regularly. And if you want, you can come to my classroom, too.'

Sundri looked at the supplies and listened to his loving words with the joyfulness of a blind person who had just been blessed with eyesight.

She flew back home, ecstatic.

19

'BABA! BABA!! LOOK AT what I've got', Sundri shouted as she showed Rodu all the study material she had been given. 'You were saying that they would beat me, but they told me I must study, that they'll teach me. They gave me all these things. Look here… this beautiful *takhti*, this book of alphabets, two *kalams*, an inkpot, and here's *gaachni* for my *takhti*. Have you seen everything? I'm going to write now!'

Rodu wondered who could have given these objects to Sundri. He became suspicious. 'Where did you get all this from? Return it wherever you stole it from. This will all end with my head getting bashed in.'

'No, Baba! I swear by the Devi, Giani ji gave me all these things. Come with me, I'll prove it to you.' She took Rodu's hand and pulled it.

The determination and fearlessness on Sundri's face convinced Rodu. And when she told him how the entire incident had unfolded, he did not doubt that she told the truth.

From that day on, Sundri was allowed the privilege of receiving an education in the village. She spent whatever time she could spare after her daily chores to study. Even while sleeping, her mind thought of her lessons. She went to Giani ji every day for an hour or two to learn. Even though Giani ji wanted her to sit alongside the other students, he made a separate sitting arrangement for her outside the classroom to avoid any hindrance to her learning. It worked well for Sundri because the other children wouldn't have let her learn anything if she had sat with them. But even then, they soon began bothering her. The students bullied her while coming in or going out of the classroom. One girl pushed another so that she fell over Sundri. Now deemed untouchable, the girl who fell chased the other girls to make them untouchable, too. Someone toppled Sundri's inkpot with a slight touch of their foot. Someone else peeled off a layer from her *kalam*, bent it like a bow and then hurled it at her face. Their taunts were never-ending, but Sundri never complained. She concentrated on her studies.

But there was another obstacle in her way – the belligerent attitude of the wealthy villagers. They sometimes threatened Giani ji to abstain from the changes he brought to the village.

The matter finally came before the villagers one day when they had gathered at Chanda Singh's haveli after his mother's demise. The conversation eventually moved to the reforms in the village. Jwala Singh mentioned that government doctors had purified the village well with some medicine. 'It's for our benefit only', Sunder Singh explained. 'That day, Jeeva Singh's son, Bachan Singh, said that the medicine kills the bacteria and germs in the water.'

Natha Singh raised his eyebrows, causing his turban

to move further up his forehead. 'What nonsense! It's these medicines that cause diseases. Don't you know what happened with the plague outbreak a few years ago? The British authorities scattered some tablets everywhere. The rats died after eating them, but their odour caused the plague. So many people died.'

'How would uneducated people like us know of such things,' Sunder Singh replied. 'We believe what we're told. Only literates can understand such explanations.'

'Listen', Baba Bhan Singh said, 'I've seen many educated people, and you might feel bad about hearing the truth, but I can't digest this. Jeeva Singh hasn't accomplished anything by getting his son educated. In fact, that's what made the boy go insane. These young men waste no time in mixing with people of lower castes. Last night, Varyama said that the old Giani ji has started teaching the girl of a low-caste *kalandar*.'

'Yes, Varyama is right', another man spoke, 'I've seen her sitting near the gurdwara many times. I thought of talking to Jeeva Singh about it and getting an explanation from Giani ji, too, but I thought maybe it's best to avoid such arguments. Jeeva Singh is already bedridden and in bad health; it's not good to cause a patient more trouble. But this is not right. Today, she's going to the gurdwara; tomorrow, it will be the village well.'

A second man piped up, 'Yes, you're right. These people won't mend their ways. There was a bloody massacre in Rawani village for the same reason. The Khalsa community kept trying to "cleanse" and "reform" the village.'

A third man added, 'Brothers! I think it's best to speak the truth to their faces. There's still time; things haven't gone too far yet. But if that Giani ji is not kept in check, something like the Rawani incident will happen here, too. They say, "One and one make eleven". Earlier, there was only Bachan Singh, but now this Giani ji has come to support him.'

And then a fourth one went, 'Yes, I agree. And Bachan Singh had that poor Pala Singh thrown behind bars as well. Now, what do we have to do with all that? He will come here every day and tell us to send our kids to the school.'

A fifth man, 'Now, tell me, it's been quite some time, and how much has he really taught our kids by now? Earlier, they used to help at home; now that's also finished. See, brothers, I'm not sending my girl to that school again. What's the use of a gold ring in your ear if it hurts?'

A sixth man said, 'Yes, brother! If you aren't sending your child to school, then why should anyone else? I would rather throw those *takhti*s into the well. Earlier, my girl did all the work around the house. But ever since she joined the school, she doesn't do anything. She merely sits in a corner holding that stick in her hands.'

A seventh man added, 'Everything would've been settled by now if Pala Singh was here.'

An eighth man went, 'Brothers! I don't want to say anything openly, but everyone knows the truth. Who else can be behind Pala Singh's arrest...'

Another one quipped, 'Let it be! Pala Singh's sentence is short. He'll probably be released even sooner due to his appeal. And the moment he is out, truth and lie will be filtered out automatically. Why should we bother?'

The conversation continued for some time, but no one arrived at any conclusion because the bigwigs of the village, Pala Singh and his men, were still in jail.

20

AFTER BEING ILL FOR a year and a half, Jeeva Singh finally completed the journey of life and left the world. The entire responsibility of the household now fell on Bachan Singh. His mother passed her days only for his sake; she did not have any other children.

Meanwhile, Pala Singh and his gang, as well as Bhai Dasondha Singh, were all set free one by one upon completion of their sentences. While in jail, they had heard that Bachan Singh had appointed a new *Granthi* to the gurdwara. So, the first thing they decided to do upon their return was to get him expelled from the village. Although they got arrested due to Bhai Dasondha Singh's statement, they knew he said what he did because of his foolishness, so they pardoned him. They also knew he was a crucial tool for them, and so they called on his services, once again.

When Pala Singh returned after his release, almost the entire village gave him a warm welcome. Bhai Dasondha Singh's importance and prestige had also increased at least ten times by then. 'See, the retribution Bachan Singh got for trapping the saintly Bhai ji for no reason?' everyone said. 'His father died immediately afterwards. We must be afraid of

God. It's rightly said that a poor man's curse always proves fatal.'

The villagers soon developed a dislike for Giani ji as well. Even the families who had been favourable towards him became hostile, and many of them withdrew their children from his school. Saddened by all of it, Giani ji finally decided it was best to remove himself from the situation, and one day, he left the village. He did not listen to Bachan Singh's request to stay, insisting that his presence would only disturb the peace and harmony of the village.

Thus, even though Pala Singh and his men had anticipated some trouble in removing Giani ji, Bhai Dasondha Singh resumed his duty at the gurdwara with ease.

The number of devotees had increased manifold since Giani ji took charge of the gurdwara, and the men started planning how to attract even more people to outdo him. They also wanted to win the confidence of Giani ji's followers.

Guru Nanak Dev Ji Gurpurab was drawing near, and they decided to arrange for the services of a *Ragi Jatha* (a group of the members who sing and/or play musical instruments while reciting or singing *Gurbani Kirtan* together as a team).

When he returned to the village, Bhai Dasondha Singh immediately spread the word that Bachan Singh had bribed the officials and forced him to make damaging statements before the court. And so, as the villagers' respect for the *Granthi* increased, their dislike for Bachan Singh deepened. A chatter spread in the village about excommunicating him for his increasing involvement with the juggler's girl. The villagers accused him of visiting Rodu's cottage every day for hours on the pretext of teaching the girl. Ultimately, it was decided to put forth the issue before the entire community at the gurdwara on Gurpurab. After discussing everything in detail, a unanimous decision would be made.

By now, Sundri had been completely transformed. The company of Giani ji and Bachan Singh, along with her untiring studies, had sharpened her. She had become familiar with the Sikh way of life, history and literature.

Bachan Singh's mother was a traditional woman, and the neighbourhood women did their best to provoke her by liberally sprinkling masala on their already exaggerated stories about Bachan Singh. But Bachan Singh and Giani ji had already explained everything to her, and she remained unaffected by the gossip.

With Gurpurab approaching fast, Sundri got desperate to attend the event. She was awash with reverence, having learned all about the Sikh gurus, their contributions, and sacrifices from Giani ji. The fear that she would not be allowed to witness the grandeur of the celebrations pierced her heart. Most of this fear had been instilled in her by Rodu. He had repeatedly told her that they could not enjoy the privileges of high-caste society. As 'untouchables', they weren't allowed to enter places of worship. But still, she yearned to enter the gurdwara on Gurpurab and pay obeisance somehow.

Just one day was left before the Gurpurab celebrations began, and preparations were in full swing. Sundri found out that a *Ragi Jatha* would perform *kirtan* the next morning. All night, she had tried to think of the best way to sneak into the gurdwara. Living in the company of a monkey her whole life, she had developed the skill of one herself. She thought of slipping into the gurdwara early morning when the entrance gate opened and escaping the eyes of the attendants by climbing the thick branch of a tree inside the courtyard. At the same time, she was scared of getting caught. *Would I sit at a higher place in the presence of the Guru?* she thought; *I must think of a plan so that no one can spot me.*

She went to sleep that night with several ideas running through her head.

When she woke up, it was bright outside. She cursed herself for sleeping till late in the morning.

She couldn't stay in the hut for a moment longer. Rodu was still snoring loudly, fast asleep. She stepped out of the hut carefully, without making any noise, and went straight towards the gurdwara. She expected to hear the music of *vaaja jori* to reach her ears from afar, but she was wrong. The main gate of the gurdwara was still closed. That's when she joyfully figured out that the light shining down was from the moon. It wasn't dawn like she had feared.

Still planning how to get inside, she suddenly thought of the small storeroom in the courtyard of the gurdwara, used to store husk and fodder. It was often left unlocked, and its door opened into the room where the Guru Granth Sahib was.

The brightness of the moon made her nervous because she feared someone might see her, but she was determined.

Concentrating on what she needed to do, she went to the back of the gurdwara premises. She saw a trough next to a small room, near the main building. She jumped onto the edge of the trough, and then, balancing her toes on some protruding bricks, scaled the wall of the room and climbed onto the roof with the agility of a monkey.

Once at the roof, she grabbed the thick branch of a tree, swung on it and landed in the courtyard. She quickly entered the storeroom and hid in a corner. She pushed gently on the door to the room with the Guru Granth Sahib. It opened, and a part of the straw fodder pressed against the door spilt into the room.

Sundri panicked but didn't lose heart. Three or four men were sleeping in the room, and no one woke up by the sound. A streak of moonlight shone into the otherwise dark room through a window. She rushed out, found a small rug and started collecting the spilt fodder.

After labouring for an hour, she could make enough space to stand inside the storeroom. A giant heap of fodder was behind her. She moved the fodder to the other side, closed the door, sat behind it and dozed off.

She thought of the parables about Guru Nanak that Bachan Singh had told her, and they began to appear like they were actually unfolding before her eyes. On that day, and at that moment, the divine Guru had entered the world. She could see…

There was a big celebration at Rai Bhoi di Talwandi, where Guru Nanak was born. Kalu Patwari's home was decorated with thousands of lights at the birth of his son. The air was full of the fragrance of all the flowers in the world. The moon, capable of brightening the darkest of hearts, was shining in the lap of Guru Nanak's mother, Tripta. Anyone who glanced at the child felt a strange heavenly light within.

Then Sundri watched the child playing hide-and-seek and sleeping under the cool shade of trees. She saw a snake sheltering the divine child with its hood. Deeply lost in her thoughts, she fell at the Guru's feet and washed his feet with her tears. 'My Lord!' she said, 'Please turn your ethereal eyes towards me and tell me what crime I have committed for which I'm denied the right to place my head at your feet. I have escaped many eyes to reach here. Master of my heart, play hide-and-seek with your friends, but not with me; do not stop me from coming to you. A poor person like me is not powerful enough…'

She heard a sound coming from the sky, melodious and heavenly. The soul-stirring strains of a musical instrument echoed in the air. It scented everything around. She saw the Guru descending from the heavens with two companions. They landed in a valley surrounded by beautiful flowers that swayed with joy. The Guru positioned himself on a throne, with his companions to his left and right.

In this world of dreams, Sundri ran to hold his feet. She pleaded, 'Master of my heart! Don't leave me now… Don't stop me from coming near your feet. Stop those who are obstructing my path instead. My Lord! Don't break my heart.'

She felt the Almighty moving His hand on her head. 'Sundri! I'm glad to be with you,' she heard, 'no one can stop you… Now get up and listen to me.'

Sundri lifted her head. She was filled with a strange sensation. Every pore of her body vibrated. Words dipped in heavenly nectar echoed in her ears as if all the musical notes of the world had formed a singular wondrous chorus. The companion on the Guru's right sang to the melody of the *rabab* played by the companion on the Guru's left.

Har amrit bhinney loeinaa
mann prem ratannaa raam raajae,
Mann raam kasvattee laaeiaa kanchan sovinnaa.
Gurumukh rang chalooliaa meraa mann tann bhinnaa,
Jan Nanak musak jhakoliaa sabh janam dhan dhannaa.

(My eyes are wet with the Nectar of the Lord, and my mind is imbued with His Love, O Lord O King.
When the Lord applied His touchstone to my mind, it was found to be one hundred per cent gold.
As Gurmukh, I am dyed in the deep red of the poppy, and my mind and body are drenched with His Love.
Servant Nanak is drenched with His fragrance; blessed, blessed is His entire life.)

Sundri's eyes opened. She found herself sitting in the storeroom with husk all around her. From the partly ajar door, she saw that the *Ragi Jatha* had started reciting verses from *Asa ki Var*, composed by Guru Nanak.

Sundri sat cross-legged, savouring the *kirtan*. She saw the sacred Guru Granth Sahib for the first time that day. But she didn't know how to go inside and bow her head before it. The yearning distracted her, but as long as the *kirtan* went on, Sundri's heart remained full of fervour and ecstasy.

The sun was brightening. Only the last four or five verses of the *Var* were left, and a couple of devotees had entered the hall. Sundri wished that the day would stretch into a year and she could remain absorbed in the benign presence of the Guru. Even Brahma or Vishnu would not deter her from savouring it.

When it was almost time for the *bhog*, one of the *Ragi* Singhs went to Bhai Dasondha Singh. 'Bhai Sahib Ji, it's time for the *bhog*, and the devotees haven't turned up yet,' he whispered.

The *Granthi*, who had been dozing off, woke up with a start and rubbed his eyes. 'What did you say?' he asked.

The *Ragi* Singh repeated himself. 'They're village people, after all', Bhai Dasondha Singh said, 'I'll go and get them,' and he went out to gather some villagers.

The *Ragi* Singhs were stretching out the *kirtan* to attract more devotees before starting the *bhog*. Bhai Dasondha Singh went to the village once, then twice, and again for a third time.

By noon, when the aroma of *karah parsad* had spread all over the village, the gurdwara was filled with men, women, and children.

But after sitting in the gurdwara for just a few minutes, they began getting impatient. Some started gently elbowing the *Ragi* Singhs, signalling them to finish the singing. 'Hurry up with the *bhog,* we've got to tend to our field', they whispered. At last, the *bhog* concluded, and Bhai Dasondha Singh came forward confidently to perform *ardas*. Large quantities of *karah parsad* had been prepared. Pala Singh and his buddies had offered eleven rupees for it, besides a similar offering from the panchayat.

With the concluding words of the *ardas,* '...*Nanak naam chardi kala, tere bhaane sarbat da bhala...*' the entire *sangat* bowed their head before the Guru Granth Sahib.

Suddenly, the door of the storeroom burst open with a loud bang and a large heap of fodder spilt into the room. Along with it, a girl fell face forward at the spot marked for bowing one's head before the Guru Granth Sahib.

Everyone in the hall turned to see what had happened. When the girl came out from under the fodder, and the villagers realized it was the juggler Rodu's daughter, they became furious.

The villagers began thrashing the girl with slaps, punches, and kicks. They were already fed up with the ongoing tension in the village due to her, and now all the *karah parsad* had become impure because of the presence of the Untouchable girl inside the Gurdwara. It was now ruined and would become a meal for birds and stray dogs.

The villagers were hell-bent on punishing the girl but restrained themselves thinking of the possible dire consequences of unleashing their fury. They did not want to face yet another court case after what had happened with Pala Singh.

They dragged the poor girl out into the courtyard, cursing her. She was bleeding profusely from the nose, mouth and head. Her clothes were drenched in blood. Some of the villagers wondered if the girl had died after such a severe thrashing and began to whisper among themselves.

When Bachan Singh arrived at the scene, the villagers' rage intensified. They had been trying to find an excuse to humiliate him, and now they had the perfect opportunity. Some of them openly questioned his character and accused him of being the culprit behind what had happened with Sundri at the gurdwara.

But Bachan Singh did not care. When he noticed Sundri drenched in blood and lying unconscious, a balloon of courage grew inside him, and his blood began to boil. 'Why has she been beaten!' he shouted, 'What wrong did she do?'

Just one question from Bachan Singh made dozens of tongues wag,'Why was she here…? Who brought her here…? Our religion has been contaminated… It is a sign of the arrival of *Kalyug*… All the *karah parsad* is spoiled…'

Shouting and moving away from Sundri, the villagers encircled Bachan Singh and stared at him like a cat savouring a mouse before killing it.

But Bachan Singh's anger was unabated. Trembling with fury, he shouted, 'This is the height of ruthlessness. If this poor girl entered the gurdwara to pay obeisance and listen to *shabad kirtan* out of her devotion to the Guru, then what is wrong with that? She has been thrashed so mercilessly that...' Bachan Singh felt a lump in his throat, and tears welled in his eyes as he spoke.

His words were futile. It was like preaching before drunkards in a bar. The villagers started jeering at him. One of them stepped forward and said, 'What did you say? She had come to listen to *shabad kirtan*? Sardar ji, go and tell these tall tales to someone else!'

'A sly thief!' another one said.

Then a third one, 'We knew he would show his real face one day. After all, a lie has no legs to stand on. Nobody can hide their sin for long.'

And a fourth one, 'This fool thinks everyone will fall for his tricks like Giani ji. But he doesn't know our Bhai ji won't allow such mischief in this gurdwara.'

Bachan Singh did not understand their bizarre accusations and their hostile expressions began to worry him.

He turned to look at Sundri. He feared she would die if not attended to soon. He stepped forward quickly and lifted her into his arms. 'Cruel! Heartless!' he shouted as he left. 'Look, I'm taking her to my house. Excommunicate me, or do whatever you want. I have nothing but disgust for all of you.'

They heckled him as he left, shouting whatever came to their minds at the moment.

After some time, their rage subsided. When a man sees his enemy trapped in a new web, he considers even his loss as gain. Besides, they need not do anything about Bachan Singh; their purpose has been achieved.

The *sangat* settled back inside the Gurdwara. The *sewadars* cleared the spoiled *karah parsad* from the hall and prepared a fresh batch to distribute. How and where did they dispose of the spoiled *parsad*? Only God knows.

The day had progressed, and the devotees were getting impatient to return home when the younger son of Lambardar Natha Singh entered the gurdwara. He was followed by a pure-bred puppy wagging its tail. The boy sat near his father. As soon as the puppy saw Natha Singh, it jumped into his lap and tried to lick his mouth. Maybe it had smelled the *karah parsad*. Natha Singh patted its back while gently pushing its head down, cradling the puppy like a small child.

Jwala Singh, sitting next to Natha Singh, extended his arm to pet the puppy. 'Lambardar!' he exclaimed, 'Where did you get this dog from? He seems to be of a fine breed.'

Natha Singh was more than ready to talk about the puppy. 'I got him after a lot of effort', he said. 'Tehsildar Tek Chand and my father have been good friends for many years. Last year, before leaving for England, Tek Chand's boss gave his pet bitch to him. She hadn't even conceived when my father booked this puppy. I had to go to Tek Chand's place five or six times with repeated requests for the puppy and paid twenty-five rupees for him. He's really intelligent. My father said once when Tek Chand's buffalo was stolen, the puppy's mother helped catch the thief.'

Daya Singh, sitting close by, patted the puppy's head. 'If he remains alive, he'll certainly fight a lion one day. See, how strong he is!'

'I've arranged for him half a kilo of meat daily and as much milk as he can drink.' Natha Singh stuck four fingers into the dog's mouth and continued, 'See, he doesn't bite no matter what I do to him. But if he sees a stranger at home, he barks at the top of his voice and jumps up and down to free himself and pounce on whoever it is.'

The fresh batch of *karah parsad* was being distributed among the devotees. Natha Singh fed the puppy its share, and then gave it another third of his share, before eating the rest of the *parsad*.

Once the *parsad* had been distributed, the topic of collecting money for the *Ragi Jatha* came up.

Bhai Dasondha Singh got up and addressed the *sangat*. 'Khalsa Ji! The *Ragi* Singhs have recited a moving *kirtan*. Now it's our duty to honour them with offerings and seek blessings of the Almighty.'

Lambardar Ladha Singh, being a leader, had been made to sit in the front row, and all eyes were glued on him now, curious about how much money each of them was offering. For some time, they egged each other on, 'You should be the first..., no you, no you...".' until finally, Ladha Singh took out a half-rupee coin from the folds of his turban and placed it before the *Jatha*. The *Ragi* Singhs were disappointed to see such a paltry amount. On the other hand, Deva Singh, the carpenter, offered one rupee.

Ladha Singh was furious at Deva Singh, aghast that the low-caste carpenter had offered more money than the village head. *Is he trying to lower my prestige before the community?* He felt like teaching the carpenter a lesson but thought it best to wait until an appropriate occasion.

But soon, Babu Karam Singh, a practical and truthful man from the village, spoke up, like he always did in the face of wrongdoing. 'Lambardar!' he lashed out, 'Aren't you ashamed of offering only half a rupee to the *Ragi* Singhs? You should've thought of your position in the community. After all, you're one of the village heads. Look at Deva Singh, he has graciously offered one rupee.'

Ladha Singh had managed to bear the first blow to his dignity with some difficulty, and now another one had struck him. 'Listen here, Karam Singh!' he shouted, 'I've told you many times to think before you speak. If one doesn't have any sense himself, he should seek it from others. Have you forgotten the time when Dayala Baniya was going to forfeit your assets, and you were crying and begging in front of my father for help with your turban at his feet? If he hadn't helped, you would've been ruined by now.'

Both of Babu Karam Singh's sons were sitting close by. Seeing his father being insulted, Bela Singh sprang up. 'Look here, Lambardar! Control your tongue. My father is not like that potter Fajju whom you swindled out of his money and then had him thrown into jail. You've spoken enough filth already, but don't you dare utter another word against our father. One's respect is always in one's own hands.'

Lambardar Ladha Singh was about to say something when his nephew Fauja Singh jumped in, 'That's enough, you dirty little pig! Don't get too big for your shoes. We've said everything we wanted, and we'll say it a hundred times more. Do what you want. We're successful because of our hard work, not because someone gave us anything.'

'How about you stop talking rubbish?' Karam Singh's younger son said. 'The grandfather dies of starvation, but the grandson still behaves like a king, haan.'

'Don't you dare compare yourself to us!' Lambardar Ladha Singh shouted.

A friend of Karam Singh joined the fight. 'Of course, how can anyone compare themselves to you? Most of your wealth came from your in-laws, and you got the rest by selling off your daughters. And still, you try and show off. Have you forgotten the day when all three of your brothers were caught in a robbery case, and your father was dragging his feet from door to door, begging for help? If we hadn't come to your rescue, those men would have auctioned off even the clothes of your women.'

'That's enough, you mongrel!'

'Shut up, you son of a bitch.'

'Catch him, where does he think he's going?'

'Who the hell has the balls to touch me?!'

'Oh, yeah?'

'Yeah!'

'Take this, then!'

'Bring it!'

Within minutes, the gurdwara hall had become a battlefield. Thankfully, no one was carrying weapons in a place of worship, otherwise, who knows how much blood would have been shed that day. Although the villagers used the musical instruments of the *Ragi* Singhs to attack each other, they weren't strong enough to knock someone down. Instead, they crumpled and fell to the floor after hitting their targets.

Bhai Dasondha Singh hid under a divan. The *Ragi* Singhs ran away barefoot after hurriedly collecting their offerings and heaved a sigh of relief when they reached the railway station.

The police reached the spot by the evening, and rounded up everyone young and old.

And what was the result? As usual, most of the villagers' money went into lawyers' pockets, some was spent at the court proceedings, and the rest went into the claws of the police.

21

BACHAN SINGH'S DECISION TO take Sundri to his house came with plenty of challenges. His mother, who had already heard all kinds of tales about Sundri, almost lost her mind when she saw Bachan Singh carrying the bloodstained girl. It was a difficult time for her. She couldn't utter a word of concern to Bachan Singh, nor could she bear to witness what was hapenning in front of her eyes. How could she let the low-caste daughter of a juggler stay at her house?

The incident became a hot gossip, spreading like wildfire in the village, and the villagers ostracised both mother and son.

Bachan Singh was not unaware of all this. He understood his mother's predicament and knew the extent to which the villagers could go against him. Despite knowing this, he had brought Sundri to his house. The first thing he did on reaching home was to call a doctor to attend to her. While the doctor examined her, Bachan Singh went to Rodu's hut to tell him what had happened and bring him to the house.

Rodu felt dizzy when he saw Sundri's condition. Then he thought of Bachan Singh, who was already paying a heavy price because of him and Sundri. Nobody knew the extent of wrath Bachan Singh would face from his community for this offence.

He fell at Bachan Singh's feet in gratitude and sought his permission to take the unconscious Sundri back, even though he knew, in the depth of his heart, that the care and treatment she was receiving at Bachan Singh's house was not possible in his hut. He couldn't even arrange for ordinary medicines there. But jeopardising Sundri's life was the only way to safeguard Bachan Singh's reputation.

Despite Rodu's repeated requests, Bachan Singh refused to let Sundri go until recovery. Even though Rodu realized it was the best thing for her, his deep attachment to Sundri made it difficult. Finally, he steeled his heart and made up his mind to leave her there for a few days.

Rodu kept visiting Bachan Singh's house for some days to stay updated about Sundri's condition, but he had to stop. Whenever he passed through the streets, the villagers heckled and harassed him.

Bachan Singh was also sailing in the same boat, but the strength of his character did not let him drift from his path. Despite the harsh criticism and recrimination at every corner, he dedicated himself to Sundri's care.

Sundri remained unconscious for two days, opening and closing her eyes occasionally. On the third day, she briefly gained consciousness three or four times and murmured something. That night, around 9 p.m., Rodu came to Bachan Singh's house, escaping the villagers' eyes and sat beside Sundri. After some time, her eyelids opened slowly, and she began to observe the objects around her. Rodu heaved a sigh of relief and, placing his hand on her forehead, said, 'Sundro!'

Sundri responded weakly, 'Yes, Baba.'

'My child, look at me.'

Sundri turned to see Rodu sitting beside the bed, near her head. She spread her arms towards him, and he moved his head forward. As she embraced him, she asked in a feeble voice, 'Baba, where am I?'

'At home.'

'No, Baba, this is not home. We don't have a bed at our home.' Once again, she looked at her surroundings in bewilderment. Then she noticed the bandages on her head, forehead and chin.

Sundri tried to reach for Rodu's face. 'Baba, who brought me—' she started to ask and then fell silent as the memory returned to her. 'Did I faint?'

'Yes, my child.'

'All right, Baba, let's go home.'

'We will, my child. But let's wait until you recover.'

'No, Baba, I'm fine!'

Sundri tried to sit up in the bed. Rodu helped her lie back down and gently stroked her head. 'Go to sleep, my child. I'll take you home early morning.'

Bachan Singh was sitting close to them. It was almost midnight. 'Sardar ji!' Rodu said to him politely with his hands joined, 'Sundri has regained consciousness. I must go now. I'll come back tomorrow morning.'

'Don't worry, Baba, you can leave now.'

Sundri seemed to have gone back to sleep. Rodu looked at her lovingly, grabbed his walking stick, and went out.

After he left, Sundri turned over on her side and asked for water. Bachan Singh brought her a glass and helped her drink.

She looked at him for a while and asked, 'Did you bring me here?'

'Yes,' he said, adjusting the bed sheet. 'Don't worry, you're recovering fast. But you shouldn't move or even talk much.'

Sundri wasn't one to listen to instructions easily, though. 'No, I'm all well,' she said. Then she looked at her hands, turning them over to look at both sides. They had become pale yellow as if stained with turmeric. 'Did *you* bring me here?' she asked again.

'Yes.'

'Why?'

'Because you were badly hurt. You had fainted.'

'And you brought me here by touching me...?'

'Is there anything wrong in touching you?'

'Yes, I'm from a low caste.'

'No, for me, you're the highest among all castes of the world. Sundri, I don't think of you as Untouchable.'

'You don't? Then how do you think of me?'

'Just like me,' Bachan Singh replied. 'Anyway, forget all that. Tell me, how did you manage to enter the gurdwara that day?'

Sundri became nervous, full of regret and sorrow about her decision. *It was my stupidity to go, that's why the Guru has punished me.*

'It was my mistake,' she said, embarrassed.

'Mistake? No, Sundri. I don't mind your going there. I'm just asking how you managed to get inside. Didn't anyone stop you?'

Sundri told him everything that had happened.

'I was listening to the *kirtan* from behind the door. When the *ardas* started, I stood up with my eyes closed and hands joined in prayer. As soon as it finished, I bowed my head before the Guru Granth Sahib, forgetting where I was. When I bent down, my head banged against the door. It opened suddenly, and a huge heap of fodder fell on me. I came tumbling into Guru Granth Sahib's room, and my forehead touched the exact spot where I wished to bow my head. Guru Sahib fulfilled my desire of bowing my head before Him, but at the same time, He punished me for my audacity.'

Bachan Singh's heart filled with love as he listened to the story of Sundri's devotion and determination. He held her hand affectionately.

'Sundri! You are so innocent; I have such great regard for you.'

Until now, Sundri believed that the only beings in the world who cared for her were Rodu and Lachho. A new hope sprang up inside her. *Bachan Singh has respect for me in his heart*. She was only fifteen and unaware of the value of love, but she was old enough to understand its tone.

Under Bachan Singh's care, Sundri began to heal quickly. Was it because of the medication or Bachan Singh's devotion for her? Nobody knows.

As Sundri progressed in her recovery, her affection for Bachan Singh deepened. For his part, Bachan Singh, too, noticed that Sundri had a heart of gold. He found himself drawn to her.

As for his mother, a woman's heart can be hard as stone in one moment and like a stream of water in another. Sada Kaur had resented the juggler's girl, but since Bachan Singh had brought her home and told her what had happened at the gurdwara, she felt sympathy for Sundri. How could anyone hate Sundri when they saw her fair and slim frame, eyes full of meaning and innocent smiling face? At the same time, the hatred directed towards her family by the villagers terrified Sada Kaur.

Over two weeks, Sundri's wounds healed, except for the gravest one on her forehead, which needed bandage for a few days more.

Bachan Singh was concerned about this wound, not because he thought it was grave, but for the scar it might leave. But to his surprise, when the bandage was removed, he found that the small arc-shaped scar further added to her beauty.

It was 10 p.m., one night. Sada Kaur had finished her chores and gone to sleep on the back verandah, where Bachan Singh's bed was.

Sundri was lost in thought while lying in her bed in a small room in the courtyard. Perhaps her ears were waiting for a knock at the door; she had to return to her hut the next day. She was desperate to speak to Bachan Singh. She did not know what she wanted to talk about, but the impending separation from him felt like a separation from her own life. She glanced at the door even when she heard the faint sound of a straw moving outside, wondering why he hadn't shown up. Sada Kaur wasn't worried, however. Sometimes, Bachan Singh didn't come home till midnight.

The clock struck eleven. Sundri couldn't lie or sit on the bed any longer. She got up and started pacing up and down.

Finally, there was a knock at the door, and she rushed to open it. Bachan Singh entered the room.

Sundri burst into laughter like a child when she saw him. 'Why are you so late today?' she asked.

Bachan Singh did not respond immediately. He sat in the chair next to Sundri's bed. She followed him and sat on the bed.

Bachan Singh could tell that Sundri was feeling the chill because of the wind. 'I'm sure you're feeling cold in this room. Come, let me shift your bed to the living room.' He helped her get up from the bed. Her hand was cold as ice.

'Sundri! Have you been wandering in the cold? Do you want to fall sick again?' Without waiting for an answer, he moved her bed to the living room, followed by the chair.

'You'll fall ill again if you're careless like this,' he said with exasperation as he helped her lie down and covered her with a quilt.

Sundri didn't say anything. When Bachan Singh touched her arm, he saw that her eyes had filled with tears.

'What's the matter, Sundri?' he asked, regretting his harsh

words. He got up from the chair, sat on her bed, and took her hands in his own. 'Have I offended you?'

But Sundri was in another world. *Bachan Singh is so concerned about me... so much love... he's worried just because of my cold hands. I'm so fortunate... no, unfortunate!*

Overcome with these thoughts, she continued crying instead of answering his question.

Bachan Singh tightened his grip on her hands. 'Sundri...' he started but was unsure what to say next. He, too, was immersed in an ocean of emotions.

Sundri did not see Bachan Singh even though he was sitting in front. She was envisioning her body lying inside her hut. Without Bachan Singh, she would be like a dead person.

She felt weak; a hollowness was forming within her. Bachan Singh had blended into her life so much that she could not imagine separation from him; she felt that if he went away from her, she would not survive.

Even as she was lost in her thoughts, Sundri felt the warmth from their tightly clasped hands spreading through her body. 'Sundri! My Sundri! Why aren't you saying anything?' she heard a voice ask, 'I have so much to talk about tonight.'

She was used to hearing 'Sundri' from Bachan Singh's mouth, but this endearment filled her with an inexpressible ecstasy.

She raised her head and looked at Bachan Singh. She noticed a depth of feeling in his eyes. It was love. Both of them stayed that way, gazing at each other for a while. When Bachan Singh finally glanced at his watch, he wondered how time could have passed so swiftly. It was half past midnight.

At last, he broke the silence by repeating, 'Sundri! I had to talk to you about so much today.'

'*Had* to...?' Sundri smiled, 'Not anymore?'

'It's past midnight!'

'All right, if you're feeling sleepy...'

'No, I'm not. I'm worried about your sleep.'

'Mine? But I won't be able to sleep tonight.'

'Why? Why won't you be able to sleep?'

Sundri kept quiet.

'Sundri!'

'Yes?'

'Are you going to leave?'

Sundri did not answer and bit her index finger instead.

'If you were to leave me one day, why did you come to me?'

Sundri took a deep breath as a reply.

'Sundri, you've filled my life with *amrit*.'

Sundri stayed quiet. But even though she did not speak, she answered all of Bachan Singh's questions with her expressions. She wanted to respond, but she could not. She could understand Bachan Singh's language but was unable to express herself. Perhaps her thoughts could not be expressed in words, so she remained silent.

The words Sundri heard from Bachan Singh were exactly what she had wanted to say. The universe has blessed women with such remarkable powers of endurance that they can preserve emotions as vast as a sea and immovable thoughts as hard as a rock in the little vessels of their hearts. Thinking that their love was impossible, Sundri had locked her tongue and blocked that storm from coming out of her mouth.

'Sundri! Are you going to speak or not?' Bachan Singh asked again. 'All right, I will leave.' He got up.

Sundri caught hold of his shirt, indicating that he should sit back down. 'Why have you come so late today?' she asked.

Although Sundri had asked the question intending to change the subject, Bachan Singh did not veer from the conversation. He resumed his position on the bed. 'The reason for my late return is *you*. After lunch, I went straight to the fields and was so lost in your thoughts that I forgot about the time. It was 10 p.m. when I returned to my senses and rushed home.'

'Thoughts of me?' Sundri asked with an astonished look on her face. 'Me?'

'Yes, Sundri.'

'You must have been thinking that bringing me to your home has been nothing but trouble for you.'

'No, nothing like that.'

'Then, what?'

'I was thinking tomorrow you'll leave.'

'Yes, so?'

'Sundri, I…'

'Go on, tell me. Why are you hesitating?'

'I cannot live without you. My heart…'

'Yes?'

'Sundri! You're too young to know the meaning of love. If you could understand it, you'd know my state of mind without me explaining it to you.'

'Why can't I understand? You and Giani ji have taught me everything. Then how could I not know the meaning of love? I know we must love everybody. It's even written in *Gurbani*, *Jin prem kiyo tin hi prabh payo.* Only one who loves can receive the Almighty's blessings.'

This simple answer stupefied Bachan Singh. 'I'm talking about a different kind of love.'

'A different kind? You never taught me about that.'

'Such things are not taught.'

'Then why don't you tell me about it?'

'Are you going to leave tomorrow?'

'Yes, Baba sent a message asking me to.'

'And what if he hadn't sent such a message?'

'Then, I wouldn't have gone.'

'Okay, but will you remember me sometimes after you've left?'

'You won't visit me?'

'No.'

'No?' Sundri felt an unbearable pain inside her. 'Why, and who will teach me then?'

'I'll make some arrangements for you.'

'I'm not going to study with anyone else.'

'And what will you do that you need to study so much? You can now read and write perfectly, and you know many *banis* from the Guru Granth Sahib.'

'But you promised to teach me up to the tenth standard.'

'If you want to study further, I'll help you get admission to a girls' school in a city nearby.'

'And, will you stay there, too?'

'Me? How can I leave my home to stay somewhere else?'

Sundri became silent as if she had said something wrong.

'Sundri, don't you want to stay with me?' Bachan Singh continued.

'With you? But would people let me stay with you?'

'Sundri! Don't you love me?'

A sweet smile danced across Sundri's lips. She rested her head on Bachan Singh's shoulder.

'You… you… I…' she couldn't complete her sentence, no matter how much she tried.

Bachan Singh, however, had an answer to his question. The adoration emanating from every fibre of Sundri's being filled Bachan Singh with unsurpassable joy.

All the words the two lovers carried in their hearts remained unspoken. They need not express themselves anymore. They felt as if they were one.

Bachan Singh looked at his watch. 'Sundri! Go to sleep now. It's late; it's half-past-two,' he said and kissed her hand. Giddy with the sensation of his lips touching her, Sundri did not even realise when Bachan Singh left.

22

THE DARKNESS OF EVENING was slowly spreading. A chilly December wind was blowing. But the hustle and bustle at the well on the outskirts of the village of Diwanpur did not seem to be affected by the harsh weather. A young boy of about thirteen was leading a pair of white bullocks around the Persian wheel, drawing water from the well. 'Hoon, hoon,' he shouted while controlling the animals. A sharp-pitched but rhythmic sound came from the movement of the pulley-block.

Several young women from the village had gathered around the well, waiting for a turn to fill their pitchers. Their children were playing nearby with balls of mud and broken pottery.

There was a cotton field near the well, although it would be better to call it a straw field because none of the plants had any cotton buds or leaves, only empty husks. The dried-out plants rustled loudly against each other in the powerful gusts of wind.

In a nearby field were beds of fully ripe radishes. The green leaves growing from the protruding heads of the snow-white radishes swayed like feather fans waving over the head of a princess.

The lush green patch of land looked magnificent amidst the dry cotton field, like a loving child playing in the lap of an old father. And when the intermittent gusts of wind hit the patch, the delicate radish plants leaned towards the cotton twigs like scared children spread their arms towards a parent.

Three men were sitting at the edge of the radish field.

One of them pulled out a soft radish and shook the dirt off it.

'So, are we ever going to get rid of Bachan Singh, or is he going to be a pain in our neck forever?' he asked.

'Pala Singh!' the second man said, 'How is this our fault? Don't make excuses now. We told you that we either spare him or kill him. That's the only solution.'

Pala Singh said, 'I was always game for this plan. But you guys are useless. You haven't been able to set that scoundrel straight yet, there's no point in expecting anything from you all.'

The third man spoke up, 'Pala Singh! You've never thought twice about the riskiest of robberies, then why are you so afraid of Bachan Singh? I don't get it.'

The men's taunts pierced Pala Singh like arrows. 'Who says I'm afraid of Bachan Singh?' he shouted. 'I swear by God, if He grants me the right opportunity, I won't hesitate to kill him. But you've seen that little shrew Sundri – how she clings to him all the time? We have to be careful while dealing with Bachan Singh. We don't want to get rid of her along with him. Listen, Sawai Singh, I want to kill two birds with one stone – we need to finish Bachan Singh, but we should catch that little shrew as well.'

'And what about that one-eyed Rodu?' Veeru added.

'Don't worry about him. Who cares about that old man? I can crush him with just a little twist of my hand. And who will even mourn him? He could die today, and tomorrow would be just like any other day.'

'Okay, enough boasting,' Sawai Singh said, 'why did you call us here? It's freezing.'

'Oh, you're feeling cold, are you? Just say you're in the mood for some booze.'

His friends smiled, licking their lips.

'I still have a bottle and a half from the last time,' Pala Singh continued, 'that should help with the cold.'

The moods of the other two men brightened immediately. 'We're all with you,' Veeru said. 'We won't rest until you become a groom.'

'Just don't forget your friends after our *bhabhi* arrives,' Sawai Singh added.

Even without a drink, Pala Singh was feeling intoxicated just by listening to their words. 'Look at the two of you. That girl is still trapped inside Bachan Singh's house, and you guys are already talking about your sister-in-law.'

'Who told you that?' Veeru said, 'That old man took her back home five days ago.'

'Oh?' said Pala Singh, surprised. 'Maybe. You know I've been visiting my relative for the last week.'

'That means you haven't seen her since she was injured,' Veeru said.

'No.'

'Uff, she's definitely worth noticing now. Her complexion has become so fair, like a blend of saffron and wheat. And she's grown in just a few days, like the tender branch of a tree. My brother, you're in for a stroke of luck if you succeed in your mission.'

'I'm mad for her,' Pala Singh said. 'I think her beauty is going to drive me crazy. You two better help me, otherwise, I'm going to climb on top of your heads and die right there.'

'With the Almighty's grace, it'll happen in a snap of your fingers', Sawai Singh said. 'But you need to worry about Bachan Singh first. We can't even touch Sundri as long as he's around.'

'Do you think he'll marry her?'

'Why do you think he's educating her?' Veeru added. 'He's not a fool.'

'I don't know why Bachan Singh is so interested in her', Pala Singh continued. 'Is he short of matches from suitable girls? He's studied up to the twelfth standard. I've heard he's getting proposals from rich families. This girl is a great fit for a bachelor like me who is free from family responsibilities.'

'You're right, but that isn't good enough. It's an open battle – whoever wins takes the girl,' Sawai Singh said.

'You guys are just going in circles with all this chatter,' Veeru said. 'If we aren't coming up with an actual plan, I will head off. My legs are stiff with this cold.'

Pala Singh thought deeply for a while. 'I think we need to trick Bachan Singh into a court case of some sort, and then we can do whatever we want.'

'I was about to say the same thing, but what about that old Rodu?' Veeru asked.

Pala Singh whispered into the two men's ears, one by one. Their conversation continued for some time, and finally, once they reached a decision, they dispersed.

23

SOME TIME HAD PASSED since Sundri had left Bachan Singh's house and returned to her hut. Bachan Singh, however, visited Rodu's home frequently and continued her education.

One day, when he came home from his fields, he found his mother in a state of gloom. When he asked her what was wrong, Sada Kaur took a deep breath. 'What can I say, *kaka*? Nothing is hidden from you.'

'What's the matter, Ma? Please tell me.'

'*Beta*, you know this house was full of visitors once, but now nobody likes to come here. Surain's son was here from Hoshiarpur, and he stopped by this morning to convey his regards on his way home. I offered him a glass of lassi, and he left after drinking it. Someone noticed it; when he got home, everyone jumped on him for accepting a drink from this house. No one wants to have anything to do with our family. They even got holy Ganga water from Dina Nath Brahmin's house and made him drink it. Only then was he considered purified and allowed in his home.'

Bachan Singh had been noticing this change in behaviour towards his family for a while, but he had not even imagined in his wildest dreams that things would get this bad. It hurt him to see his mother's sorrow and the cruelty of his own community. 'So what, Ma? If they don't want to be associated with us, then let them stay away. We don't need any help from them to eat and live.'

'We don't, but one has to maintain some self-respect within the community. A *koonj* (a migratory bird *demoiselle crane* that specifically visits northwestern India during the winter season) will never feel the same contentment while flying solo as it does in formation with its companions. Life comes with its joys and sorrows, and one needs to share them with the people of one's own community. One cannot survive alone in a society. I still need to make arrangements for your engagement. Earlier, people visited us all the time with suitable matches for you. They brought respectable families to our home. But now, no one likes to even look at our house. What am I supposed to do now?'

Bachan Singh had been doing what he thought was best until then, but at that moment, he realized how badly hurt his mother was. He did not have any answers to her questions. 'What should be done now?' he said, unable to meet her gaze.

'What has to be done? We can't live in peace by turning away from our community. What will we lose by kicking that juggler's girl out of our life? She's the root of all our problems. If she hadn't come to our village, there wouldn't have been any trouble.'

'Ma, what's the point of blaming that poor girl?' Bachan Singh said fervently. 'If saving the life of a destitute lower-caste girl is a crime worth punishing, then I'm ready to undergo a hundred such punishments.'

When she saw that Bachan Singh was going into a frenzy, his mother got up and busied herself with chores. Bachan Singh also left the house to clear his mind. Strolling through the streets of the village, he reached Rodu's hut. When he entered, he noticed that Rodu was not there. Sundri was home but seemed distracted and did not notice him. 'Sundri!' he called out from the doorway, 'what deep thoughts are you lost in today?'

'Oh! You've come. I was waiting for you.'

Bachan Singh looked at her face and realized that she had been crying. 'Sundri! What's wrong?' he asked, worried.

She did not say anything. Bachan Singh grew more concerned. 'If you feel uncomfortable, I won't ask you, but…'

'Why would I be uncomfortable in telling you anything?' Sundri said, forcing a smile. 'Our monkey, Lachho, is lost.'

'Lost? How? Was she left out somewhere?'

'I don't know', Sundri said, taking a deep breath, 'She never goes anywhere alone. I'm sure someone has stolen her. We haven't seen her since yesterday. Baba hasn't been eating anything and was crying all night. He's been away looking for her since early morning and…'

'And what?'

'He was supposed to go to your house, but I told him not to go. I knew that you would come here.'

'Why? What else is wrong?' Bachan Singh asked urgently.

A cloud of gloom crossed Sundri's face, and her eyes became moist. Bachan Singh pulled a handkerchief from his pocket and wiped her tears. 'Sundri! Tell me quickly, what's the matter?'

'Baba was saying...' Sundri took the handkerchief from Bachan Singh's hands and wiped her eyes. 'He was saying we'll leave this place.'

'Leave?' Bachan Singh asked with surprise, 'Where would you go?'

'To some other colony.'

'But, why?'

Sundri folded and wrapped the corner of the handkerchief over her finger as if staying busy in that exercise would make her forget her troubles. She looked up to answer Bachan Singh's question, but her words stuck in her throat.

Bachan Singh held her finger and tugged on it gently. 'Tell me, Sundri... tell me, immediately.'

'People don't want us to live here anymore,' she said with a heavy sigh.

'What are you saying? Why?'

'They have started troubling us every day.'

Though Bachan Singh had not fully understood what Sundri was trying to say, he did not have the nerve to hear anything more. He tried to divert Sundri's attention. 'But why have they taken your monkey away?'

Sundri, too, felt relieved at the change in subject. 'How would I know?'

Rodu entered the cottage just then. Bachan Singh bowed

his head respectfully and stepped aside. When he asked about the monkey, Rodu burst into tears. He could not speak a word.

Sundri sprang up and threw her arms around Rodu's neck. 'What's the matter, Baba?' she asked, breathing rapidly.

'Sundri', Rodu wiped his tears with a corner of his kurta, 'Sundri, your Lachho is dead.'

Sundri let out a loud cry. 'How did it happen, Baba?' she asked, shaking Rodu by the shoulders.

'Someone threw her in the well.'

'In the well? No! It is so cruel…'

Both of them were crying now. Like a jeweller observing two objects at a time with a loupe, Bachan Singh could feel the pain of both Rodu and Sundri simultaneously.

After weeping for some time, when the old man felt lighter in his heart, he turned to Bachan Singh with his hands joined in prayer, 'Sardar ji, you've done so much for us. I cannot repay you even if I was to have a hundred births. You've transformed my child into an educated and capable person. I can't find the right words of gratitude for the troubles you've faced to save her life. I would have liked to spend the rest of my life in your service, but destiny no longer wants us to stay here. So please, bless us with your permission to settle somewhere else.'

Rodu's words pierced Bachan Singh's heart. 'But why, Baba ji?' he said with a lump in his throat.

'I don't know what to say, Sardar ji.' Rodu looked at Sundri. 'I've raised this girl with extreme hardships. She was just a baby when I brought her here.'

After telling him how he had found Sundri, Rodu continued, 'I don't know what kind of attachment people have with their biological children, but my love for Sundri is beyond explanation. When she was a small child, I was worried about her upbringing. But, she's not a child anymore; she's a grown-up girl. And I… I'm just a wretched beggar. I can't protect her.'

Rodu started sobbing. 'There's been a change in the villagers' behaviour towards us in the last several months. Every night, hooligans gather around our hut. They dance and shout and harass us. Their taunts make my blood boil. They drag your name into it as well…'

Bachan Singh was already upset with the attitude of the villagers, but he forgot all his sorrows as he listened to Rodu. 'I'm so sad to hear about all this, but I can't think of a solution immediately. Please tell me what you've decided?'

'To leave from here,' Rodu said, wiping his tears. 'Sardar ji, I don't know what to say. I wouldn't have left this place until my last breath if I wasn't so concerned about Sundri. I'm so attached to this place, to this little hut. I don't know what state I will be in when I leave, but what can I do? I have a young daughter at home – I'm worried about her.'

After a pause, Rodu continued, 'At the same time, Sardar ji, it is difficult for me to protect this gem. How can I stomach her marrying some juggler like me after the education she's gotten? I wish she gets a groom who is the right match for her, but we're not that fortunate.'

Bachan Singh was deep in thought. At last, he concluded. 'Baba ji! I won't let you go.'

Rodu stayed silent. Bachan Singh spoke, 'God did not create Sundri to let her down like this. I want her to study more.'

Rodu listened to Bachan Singh like a prisoner offered a ray of hope by a lawyer after being sentenced to life imprisonment. His heart beat loudly in his chest as he said, 'Sardar ji, you've already supported us so much and faced so much trouble. I wish for the prosperity of your family, but please don't be worried about me anymore. Let the Almighty decide – I will accept whatever is my fate. Please don't bother about us and let us leave.'

Bachan Singh drew himself up. 'But, Baba Ji, I cannot tolerate this.'

Rodu said with a heavy heart, 'If you think it best, I'll...'

Bachan Singh held the old man's hand. 'Everything will be all right.'

'But you've heard what's been happening here...'

'It's because of Sundri's presence in this village. I'll have her admitted to a school in the city.'

Sundri, sitting quietly until now, looked at Bachan Singh with a smile, like a patient hurtling towards death who had been restored to health. He answered with a smile and left.

24

RODU WAS RIGHT. THE trouble had all been due to Sundri's presence in the village. The day she left Diwanpur, almost all gossip came to an end. Pala Singh, however, was bereft. Here, he had been conspiring to have Sundri as his own, but now he was deprived of even seeing her shadow.

He had already harboured a deep hatred for Bachan Singh, but now he was beside himself with rage. Bachan Singh had taken away his prize. He became obsessed with bringing Sundri back to the village. But could he make that happen?

At last, after great deliberation, Pala Singh decided the only way Sundri would leave her studies and return was if Rodu or Bachan Singh were in some serious trouble.

He set about laying his trap, and it took three years for his efforts to yield results.

Having enrolled Sundri at Kanya Ashram in Lahore, Bachan Singh felt like he had been relieved of a huge responsibility. Unaware of the schemes of Pala Singh and his men, he thought the tribulations had ended, at least for the moment.

At the same time, he felt the pain of being separated from Sundri. It was as if something precious had gone missing from his life. Besides sending money to cover Sundri's monthly expenses and fees, he visited Rodu's hut regularly to take care of the old man's needs. Rodu, too, felt the same distress at being parted from his daughter.

Sundri continued her studies for three years and returned to Diwanpur after passing her matriculation examination. How and why did she return? How did the two lovers pass these three long years without seeing each other? Readers will get the answers to these questions from their letters. These tender letters were bathed in the colours of an exuberant love. This is why, before proceeding further with this story, it is important to present them to readers. Some impatient readers may find them irrelevant; they may skip the next pages. But it is difficult to ignore these letters. They not only capture the lovers' souls but also reveal emotions vivid enough to leave a lasting impact on any human heart.

25

Kanya Ashram, Lahore

The teachers at school are taking good care of me. All the girls in my class love me like a sister. Even the superintendent pays special attention to me. I'm not facing any problems here, but despite having everything, I feel an emptiness within myself. It's as if something precious is lost and all my being is looking for it. Please, tell me, why this is happening and what the solution for this loss is.

My heart sinks all the time, but now, while writing to you, I feel peaceful. I wish I could write to you like this forever, but then I think about something else and stop. I desperately keep waiting for your letter. Please convey my regards to Baba. I don't need to mention that the Almighty and you are the only ones to care for him.

Sundri

Diwanpur

Dear Sundri,

Your letter arrived just when I was thinking about you with great worry. What kind of worry? I can't say. I cannot even say whether I felt happy on receiving your letter. I'm unable to understand my own state of mind. The way you felt while writing to me is exactly how I felt while reading your letter. It upsets me to hear about your sadness. But there is nothing new in that. The memory of our loved ones usually makes us sad when we go somewhere else. Especially someone like you, who has never lived away from home, is likely to feel this in a new place. I hope you will soon forget the streets of Diwanpur. I know your deep attachment to your father is also responsible for your state of mind.

Still, I ask you to concentrate on your studies. Sundri! You are not a child anymore; you should know your priorities. I want you to be educated and have an identity of your own, so that your in-laws feel proud of you when you get married. Your husband should also feel proud that Sundri is not just a beautiful goddess but a beacon of talent and intellect as well.

Your Baba is doing fine here. Do not worry about anything.

Bachan Singh

Kanya Ashram, Lahore

I just received your letter. I had been waiting for it since I dropped mine in the letter box. What can I say about how I feel after reading your letter? Before I started writing, I thought it would run into many pages. But now that I'm writing it, I cannot find the right words. I have written and torn up several pages. I don't know what is holding my pen back.

You say you can't tell me why you are worried. But I am not a child, as you mentioned. I know the reason. It is me. I know that you have faced innumerable problems because of me. For saving the life of an orphaned girl, improving her standing in society, helping her get an education... you have suffered a lot. I can never repay you for that.

You have put your own life in ten times the danger that you saved me from. And I do not even know what other problems await you because of me. Do you think I don't understand these things? Who wouldn't be worried in such circumstances?

Whenever I think of all this, I feel like ending my life to stop causing any more worries and sorrows for you. But I am still dragging my feet.

You wrote that I am sad because I'm in a new place. It is not true. Every place that has the shade of your protection over me, even if it is a volcano, is heaven for me. Trust me, this is not the cause of my sadness.

You ask me to forget the streets of Diwanpur? Forgive me

for saying this, but I think you've uttered these words just to cause me pain. I cannot forget Diwanpur, not just in this life but a hundred lifetimes. The love for a father is not an ordinary thing either…

My heart sank when I read the last lines of your letter. I have not even thought about my marriage yet. Will I really have to see all my dreams and desires go to waste? I assure you I shall not remain alive to see such a day. Have you been rescuing me the whole time only to finally throw me into the fire?

I have more to write about this, but I am still in my senses, so I won't do something this foolish. I will conclude this here.

Sundri

Diwanpur

Dear Sundri,

I received your letter. I was stupid, and I feel so ashamed for hurting your feelings. Until now, I thought I was doing a noble thing. But I was wrong. The flower that I never allowed anyone to pluck so that it could retain its beauty… one that I strived to protect; why has its fragrance driven me so crazy that I started asserting my right over it?

Sundri, look how capricious the human heart is. One

moment, it is soaring high in the sky, and the next, trampled underfoot. The truth is that I wanted to hide my weakness, not only from you but myself, too. It is why I've been suppressing my feelings while writing to you. I did not want you to think of me as brutish and uncivilized.

Until now, I thought I would never reveal what lies in my heart. I thought I would hide these feelings, no matter how hard it was. But there's no stopping a broken vessel from leaking, no matter how much you repair it. I did not want to stray from my principles. That was the source of the worry and anxiety I wrote to you about, which you misunderstood. I'm also really upset with you for burdening yourself with thoughts of what I have done for you. You are doing me a great injustice, and I will never pardon you for it. Do you think I have done anything for you beyond human consideration?

But Sundri, I realized that the precious thing I was so desperate to acquire is getting attracted towards me. And just with the thought of my stepping back, there is a risk of losing the happiness of that precious thing. So why not bare my real self before you?

Sundri, you had already impressed me back when I noticed you scribbling letters on the ground outside the gurdwara but having seen your spirituality and devotion, you occupy an even larger space in my heart. I fear that I cannot remain away from you, no matter how hard I may try.

And yet, we have an obstacle in our way. I feel that the universe does not want us to be together and that we must remain separated from each other. So, would it not be better for us to step back instead of moving ahead?

Yours,
Bachan Singh

Kanya Ashram, Lahore

My dearest,

Your companionship has transformed my life and set it on a new path. Your recent letter is similar to what I wrote yesterday. While you were writing to me, I was doing the same – expressing my feelings.

Do you want to know what I was writing?

I cannot cheat you by concealing my feelings for you. It was a sin to have one thing in my heart and say another. But I won't do that anymore. You are the only person in the world whom I love so dearly. I do not know when it began, but I do know that no one except you has such a place in my heart, and no one else ever will, at least in this lifetime.

I am longing to reach a place I am not sure I really deserve. I understand it is inappropriate for me to even think of it.

And yet, despite knowing this, it is at the centre of my imagination, emotion and breath. I do not care whether I'm physically there or not. I can anoint myself just with the fragrance of that sacred place. This is the essence of my letter.

You have said there is an obstacle in our way? No, my love! Do you mean to say that marriage would be an obstacle between us? Please banish such thoughts from your mind. You must have gotten a reply from my words above; I must say that you are at full liberty to get married. In fact, I would suggest you get married at the earliest to fulfil your mother's wishes. How happy I would be to hear such news!

Yours,
Sundri

Diwanpur

Sundri,

I am so fortunate to have won the true love of a goddess. The depth of your emotions and your ethereal love have driven darkness away from my life. I feel a never-ending melody playing inside me. Every word of your letter is like a flower from a sacred garden. All worldly pleasures and comforts are nothing before it.

Sundri! I never knew that you have such nobility in your thoughts, that your heart is a whirlpool containing the love of the entire universe, that you possess such a tremendous sense of sacrifice.

I wrote in my previous letter about a hurdle between us. You have misunderstood me. Please do not ever think that I cannot marry you because of any concern about my community. I discarded such considerations long ago. I was thinking of Giani ji's teachings and my own principles. I am committed to devoting my life to social service. I am here only till my mother is alive. Later, I will dedicate myself completely to this cause.

Sundri! We live in a cruel and unjust society where innocent people are tortured and killed mercilessly. I was afraid I might drift away from my mission if I got married. I was worried that if I did not take a step back from this by controlling my emotions, I would spoil your married life, as you would have to either remain apart from me or suffer hardships with me.

But after reading your letter, all my apprehensions have disappeared. I feel ashamed of talking so naively to a person of such intelligence.

Sundri, I have the answer to all my doubts and misapprehensions. I will now only consider myself fortunate when you become mine. I will not stop even if the whole world stands in my way. I will make my way through all the hurdles and feel proud of it.

Yours,
Bachan Singh

Kanya Ashram, Lahore

My dearest!

With the stream of my life steadily flowing toward you, I feel I'm approaching a heavenly kingdom.

During the first flushes of love, we are unsure what love even means. We try to seek answers in vain. But as these doubts clear, we realize that love is a sacred and uplifting feeling that has no equivalent in the world.

My love, your magnanimity has made me richer a thousand times beyond my expectations.

It is said that everything that reaches the peak of bloom must wither after some time and that incessant laughter usually ends in crying. I feel terrified when I think of these sayings. I start trembling. My happiness has reached a point beyond my control. It is like water spilling over the brim of a vessel that is already full.

Oh, my love, an unknown worry engulfs my mind. Sometimes, it terrifies me so much that I feel my entire world crushing under it. It is like how the early morning breeze notices freshly budding flowers and starts teasing and playing with them. The delicate flowers cannot handle this bliss. They lose control. And, the next moment, that love-filled mad breeze scatters their delicate petals, and their life ends.

Save me from the clutches of this imaginary worry, my love. Keep me safe in your heart so that such thoughts don't even dare to come to me.

I am unsure what I planned to write in this letter and where I ended up. It seems either nothing more is left to be written, or there is so much to say that it cannot be finished even if I keep writing for the rest of my life. I can already see the words I want to write flashing in your eyes. So, what is left to say that has not already been expressed?

Why are you concerned about marriage, my dearest? They say that marriage makes life heavenly. If that is true, I would like to stay far away from it. I cannot even imagine a pleasure greater than your love. I have no room for more happiness.

You said you want to dedicate your life to a noble cause. My love, you are not meant to embark on this journey alone. I shall be with you. I admire your determination and your goodness in having so much compassion for society despite the cruelty and suffering you have faced. You must have been a saint in your previous life. You know those few sentences in your letter have changed my thoughts drastically? I had been concealing a darkness in my heart. I desire to take revenge on the community that tormented an innocent person, the master of my heart, a revenge so vicious that no one would ever forget.

But now my life is merged with yours; I will follow wherever you lead me. I ask once more that you take me along the difficult path you are going to tread. Be assured that I will not be an obstacle for you.

Yes, I must keep the thought of marriage at bay for now. We need to pay the price for it; we need to meditate for some time, and then we will become one forever, until the end of the world and beyond. Please do not think of my doubts expressed in this letter as baseless. Neither we nor anyone else can digest so much happiness.

Yours,
Sundri

Diwanpur

Sundri,

How will you bear the tragic news I am about to share with you? My heart is sinking, and my hands are shaking as I write this. I wish you had learned about this another way, but I must be the one to convey this to you. Sundri, your Baba… the man whose only concern was your well-being… sent you his love for the last time, and without fulfilling his heart's desire to see you, he left this world forever.

What's even more heartbreaking is that he struggled a lot before dying. He was too weak to leave his hut. The day before yesterday, when I visited him in the evening to bring him food as usual, he was crying. When I asked why he was upset, he said, 'I am desperate to meet Sundri, I'm not sure if I will live till tomorrow.'

I told him, 'Baba! Don't worry, I will go get Sundri and bring her here as soon as possible.'

But he stopped me. 'I do not want her studies to be interrupted', he told me, 'and it would not be safe for her to be here. Pala Singh has been forcing me to get him married to Sundri. He tried to persuade me many times, but when I refused point blank, he started threatening me.'

He did not speak more but gestured with his hand as if trying to tell me he was near the end. I asked him if he wanted me to convey anything to you.

He did not respond, but his glistening eyes gazed at me as if expecting an answer. I knew what he intended to ask, and I told him, 'Baba, please do not worry about Sundri; I will marry her.'

The moment I uttered these words, there was a sudden flash in his eyes, and a weak smile appeared on his lips. He lifted his hands and tried to bring them closer to each other, perhaps to thank me, but before he could do so, his arms fell onto his chest, and his head dropped towards his shoulder. It seemed as if he was holding his last breath just to hear those words of mine and die peacefully.

The police arrested Pala Singh and his companions Swaya Singh and Veer Singh, suspecting their hand in this.

Oh, Sundri! Rodu's face is still flashing before my eyes. Ever since my mother has heard this news, she, too, has not been able to control her tears. Perhaps her heart has transformed.

Everything is pre-destined, Sundri. We should never even think of taking revenge. Instead, we should be so strong that no power in this world can distract us from our path.

I understand how difficult it must be for you to read this letter. So I am not going to write any more. I ask you to face this with fortitude.

I have just come to know that Pala Singh and the others have been released on early bail. It has to be because of his money, his power and the support of the villagers. I was anticipating this.

Yours,
Bachan Singh

Kanya Ashram, Lahore

My love!

I got your letter. I cannot describe the pain I felt when I read about Baba's death. My biggest regret is that I could not be with him as he was taking his last breath. I wish he could have bestowed his blessings upon me, that I could have felt the strength of his affection one last time, his gentle hand patting me on the back. But it was not meant to be. My heart is broken. I have tried a thousand times, but I cannot console myself. I feel a surge of terrible anger inside me; it pierces my heart. But the moment I think of you, my troubled mind is eased.

Those villains did not let him live in peace, a man who could never even think of bringing harm to anyone else. And instead of ensuring punishment for their crime, some people are trying to save them. Why? Are they worried that there is a scarcity of such criminals?

My beloved! Is this the society you are so desperate to reform? Even after all this, don't you realize there is no improvement possible for those whose hearts are ablaze with crime? Are you dreaming of changing the hearts of people who are brainwashed with hate and prejudice? Do you still expect to sow seeds of reform into that barren land and see them grow?

No, no, my love! Just remove these thoughts from your mind. You cannot hit your head against this mountain and expect it to break; you will only end up bringing ruin to yourself. The only way of breaking it is to pull it out by its roots. Until all the contaminated blood from people as cruel as this is spilt until not even one single drop is allowed to remain, the generations to come will always remain infected with it.

I am sorry for writing all this in a fit of rage. I do not seem to be in my senses. These are the true feelings of my immature heart. I am trying to flush such senseless thoughts out of my mind. Perhaps I would not have done so, or I would have tried to transform them into reality to some extent if it were not for you.

I sincerely hope God will help me get rid of these violent thoughts and make me follow your principles.

My master, I do not trust my foolish mind anymore. It leads me towards destructive thoughts, and at times, a wave of such strong vengeance erupts in my mind that I lose control. I beg you to keep me safe with you.

I am so terribly upset that I cannot write more. I don't even feel like sending whatever I have written so far to you, but I am doing it. I know how broad-minded you are. I know you will forgive me for my shortcomings. Please come and take me away. I have completed my studies and am desperate to visit my Baba's home.

Yours,
Sundri

Diwanpur

Sundri,

So much anger! Such restlessness! And still, your writing is so perfect. I forget everything else while noticing the intelligence with which you craft your words. My innocent Sundri! You seem trapped in your own words when you write about how a mountain will not break by hitting your head against it… but by severing its roots. Your thoughts of revenge, of blood-for-blood, and then expecting any reform is like breaking your head against a mountain. But convincing people about moral values and winning them over through a positive approach is like excavating its roots.

At the same time, I am indebted to you for your nobility.

Even while advocating your own ideas, you are ready to follow my principles. I am confident when you become my companion in our mission, you will find these thoughts completely wrong, like calling day as night.

I can see our society is degenerating more with every passing day, but the method that you want to employ to transform it is as terrible as treating a rabid dog by bathing it.

Sundri, think of it as injecting a special medicine into patients, forcing the infected and dead white blood cells to be expelled and the alive red blood cells to take their place.

I am ready to go on this journey, and with you as my companion, we will be like one plus one that makes eleven. I will come to fetch you after five days. I have taken my mother into confidence. She will not have any objection to you working with me. But I had to adhere to her condition that until she is alive, I cannot move anywhere far away. I hope you will also prepare yourself accordingly.

We will decide our larger aim and purpose together, but for the time being, we have a small mission with which we will take a step towards our new life together. In a few days, the marriage ceremony of the daughter of Lala Rala Ram, the rich moneylender of our village, will take place. I got to know a huge amount would be wasted on lavish decorations, endless quantities of alcohol, vulgar entertainment and many other useless rituals.

Sundri! How distressing would it be to have our elders watching obscene performances by semi-nude dancers while their sisters and daughters also watch from the windows?

Would they not feel ashamed? Perhaps our intervention can avert this disaster.

There is nothing more to write now. I will be there with you in five days.

Yours,
Bachan Singh

P.S: Although I have finished the letter, a sudden thought has come to my mind. I need to applaud you. So many of your articles and stories are being published in Punjabi periodicals. I was amazed to notice them the other day when I went to the town. I am glad to see you emerge as a writer, and I am confident that one day, my Sundri will be a writer of great repute.

But, Sundri, while congratulating you on your success as a writer, I must state that there is a dire need for restraint and patience in your writing. I understand the pain of an innocent soul tormented by a cruel society, but I expect your writing to have no room for violence and harshness. Blood cannot be washed away with blood. Will you try to change this in the future?

26

THE FIRST THING SUNDRI did upon reaching the village was to pay obeisance to Rodu Baba where he had been cremated. She touched the soil of the sacred place with her forehead as a sign of her respect for him. Pieces of charred wood and ash were still lying there. For Sundri, it was not ordinary ash; her entire past lay within it. Her whole life – from being born to departing for Lahore – flashed before her eyes. Memories of Rodu pierced her heart. She wept for a long time, and only after being persuaded several times by Bachan Singh did she stop and get up.

Bachan Singh had already arranged for Sundri to stay in the nearby village of Rawani. He did not want to bring her to his own house against his mother's wishes.

Some of the residents of Rawani had opened a girls' school there and respected Bachan Singh. Having won the confidence and admiration of the villagers, Bachan Singh had chosen it as their base. Rawani was barely a mile from Diwanpur, and Sundri was soon appointed a teacher in the village school. Helping Sundri succeed at her dream job brought great relief and pleasure to Bachan Singh.

The day of the grand function at Lala Rala Ram's house

was fast approaching. He had invited the entire village. Bachan Singh had been trying for days to prevent it, but had not succeeded. Word had spread that a famous cabaret dancer from Delhi would put up a provocative performance, and the excited villagers were counting the days till the big event.

In Rawani, as Sundri arranged her things in her new home, Bachan Singh knocked at the door.

Sundri rushed to the door. 'You've been out since morning. Weren't you supposed to turn up sooner?'

Bachan Singh smiled at her. 'I've been working hard all day; I'm exhausted.' He entered the room and sat on the bed.

'Why?' Sundri asked anxiously.

Bachan Singh opened a button on his shirt and wiped the sweat from his forehead. 'I had told you about the function at Lala Rala Ram's house on Friday.'

'Yes, I remember.'

'And, today is Thursday.'

'So?'

'The function will start tomorrow.'

'Then?'

'We must be serious about our mission.'

Sundri looked at him with tenderness. 'Then what are you waiting for?'

'I do not think we will be able to stop it.'

'Why?'

'If it were only a question of persuading Rala Ram, it would not have been a difficult task, but the entire village is keen to watch that vulgar performance.'

'What are you thinking?'

'I've decided to go to Rala Ram once more; something might come out of it.'

'And where are you coming from now?'

'Not from one place; I've been breaking my head all over.'

'What has been the outcome?'

'Nothing concrete, just a timid response.'

'But why didn't you go to Rala Ram earlier? Now you'll have to go back half a mile again.'

'Meeting you isn't the only reason I've come here; I wanted to take a few reliable men.'

After a brief conversation, Bachan Singh left, leaving Sundri deep in thought.

When Bachan Singh reached Diwanpur, he went straight to Rala Ram's house. No one from Rawani had accompanied him, afraid of interfering with the affairs of such an influential man.

The arrangements for the upcoming festivities were in full swing. Tailors were stitching expensive wedding outfits. Prominent leaders from the village were being assigned tasks by Lala Rala Ram's son Dina Nath. The aroma of sweets and snacks filled the air. Young girls were singing to the beat of a *dholki*.

Pala Singh and his companions were also sitting among the village leaders. Bachan Singh's blood boiled to see them, but he tried to conceal his rage. He greeted some of the people there and sat down.

Everyone was engaged in some activity, and Bachan Singh started getting anxious. Initiating a conversation under such circumstances was not going to be easy.

As he tried to come up with a plan, he noticed Bhai Dasondha Singh walking in, his wooden slippers making a clacking sound as he moved. Although Bachan Singh was aware of the *Granthi*'s lifestyle and habits, he grew confident *Granthi* would stand by him.

Everyone welcomed Bhai Dasondha Singh with reverence, and the room echoed with requests for him to sit with them. Finding a few free moments, Rala Ram struck up a conversation with the *Granthi*. Bachan Singh seized the opportunity and went to him. 'Shah ji!' he said.

Rala Ram looked at Bachan Singh with exasperation. 'What's the matter, Bachan Singh?' he asked. Perhaps he had already heard about him from Pala Singh.

Bachan Singh grew nervous in front of Rala Ram's piercing gaze, but he mustered up the courage to continue. 'I've come to make a request,' he said. 'As you know, I don't have any selfish motive behind it. My concern is only for the welfare of this community. I humbly request you cancel the lewd performance by that woman and her troupe from Delhi. Such performances can impact the lives of our sisters and daughters.'

Rala Ram's face twisted with annoyance. 'Bachan Singh! I have already asked you not to interfere in my family's matters. And in any case, how can I stop something that is not in my hands? You know how sensitive the relationship with would-be in-laws is. Even a slight thing can cause a lifelong grudge. As they say, the taste of the engagement lasts until marriage, and the taste of marriage lasts for a lifetime. In the same way…'

He had not even finished speaking when someone jumped into the conversation. 'What's all this? Dance performances are a necessary part of celebrations when it comes to the wealthy. Bachan Singh, it's not good to cause trouble during such a happy occasion. And Shah ji only has one daughter in his community of four families. So, he must celebrate the occasion with great pomp and show.' The man looked at Bhai Dasondha Singh. 'Am I wrong?'

The *Granthi* picked at his protruding teeth with his nails, wiped his hands on his shirt and ran his tongue over his teeth. 'You're right. Such occasions don't come around every day.'

Bachan Singh turned to him. 'Bhai ji, does Sikhism teach us that a man like you should encourage a provocative performance where alcohol is openly consumed? As the head preacher of a gurdwara, how can you shirk your responsibilities?'

Bhai Dasondha Singh was left speechless, but Pala Singh interjected. 'And is it part of the teachings that you should steal the bread and butter of those poor performers? They work hard to entertain their audience. And tell me, what's wrong with drinking liquor? It's just a little homemade mixture.'

Bachan Singh did not respond, unable to respond to such nonsense. Bhai Dasondha Singh, however, was encouraged by Pala Singh's words. He scratched his belly and said, 'Alcohol is a kind of medicine. It's not a bad thing, but consuming it in excess is not good.'

Bachan Singh was beside himself with anger. He knew it was useless to argue with them, but he could not stop himself. 'All right, let's say that the consumption of alcohol is not a bad thing, that it's good instead, but could you tell me the meaning of this sentence in Gurbani, *Jhootha madh mool na peechai je ka paar vasaai*?' (Refrain from consuming the falsified alcohol. Drinking it, one forgets the Lord, and is punished in the Court of the Lord.)

Bhai Dasondha Singh rubbed his earlobe and thought for a while. 'That's right. It means that as far as possible, we should not consume alcohol. But what should one do when things get out of control?'

Despite his anger, Bachan Singh couldn't help laughing at this attempt to justify a wrong practice. He continued trying to convince them of the folly of their ways, but all his reasoning was in vain. Exasperated, he finally left.

Everyone burst into laughter the moment he stepped out. Pala Singh whispered to one of his companions, 'Veeru, did you see what that fool was up to?'

'He's trying to insult us. And it doesn't seem like he'll ever stop interfering.'

'I've had enough. You know what they say, a twisted nail can only be straightened with a hammer.'

'We need to finish this whole matter once and for all…'

Pala Singh made a threatening motion with his finger. 'Just watch. I'm going to reduce him to ashes as soon as I get the chance.'

27

IT WAS THE EVENING of the event. Everyone in the village, young and old, was heading towards the venue. Even the neighbouring villages had an abandoned air about them.

The *baraat* had arrived at a garden on the outskirts of the village around 5 p.m. as well as Anwarjan, the dancer from Delhi. Everyone who saw her got bowled over. Although she was about 35, her perfect figure and flawless make-up made her look younger than 20. Her big eyes, crimson lips and long flowing hair had captured more than a few hearts.

A large arena had been erected for the performances, with extensive seating arrangements for the guests. The groom, his elder brother, and an old pandit who advised the family were seated in the front row.

When everything and everyone was ready, the groom's brother sought the old pandit's permission to begin. 'Go ahead', he responded softly. The pandit was approaching the final phase of his life. His body had become lean, and when he walked, it looked as if he was paying obeisance to the earth. The heavy bulge of his belly had reached his thighs. The flesh below his eyes and on his cheeks had become loose, and his scalp no longer held any hair.

Suddenly, with a thunderous note from the orchestra, Anwarjan made her entrance onto the stage. It was as if the moon had appeared out of the clouds. She sang a *qawwali*, and from the very first sensuous movement of her body, Anwarjan had her audience in a trance.

Everyone cheered for her electrifying performance, but the groom's brother and the old pandit were particularly mesmerized. From the stage, Anwarjan discreetly noted who was falling for her rhythms and who was merely injured. And when she noticed that the duo she had anticipated seeing were in her thrall, she smiled coquettishly at them.

Karam Chand, the groom's brother, lost all sense at the attention. He took a ten-rupee note from his pocket and held it up for Anwarjan. The sophistication with which she accepted it only made him more obsessed with her. He discreetly handed the pandit some money, and the old man extended a note to Anwarjan. When she grazed his hand slightly while taking it from him, the old pandit felt as if he had just received an electric jolt.

Soon, money began showering at her from all sides. It was becoming difficult for Anwarjan to collect all the notes and focus on her performance. And yet, she continued singing, all the time gazing flirtatiously at Karam Chand and the pandit. Maddened with desire, they had given her all the money in their hands within minutes.

Anwarjan then started filling glasses with alcohol to serve her favourites among the audience. She offered the first glass to the pandit.

Applause and cries of 'wah wah!' rang in the air. The evening was in full swing, marked by the steady supply of drinks, the thunderous sound of the orchestra, and Anwarjan's enticing performance. Everyone, from rich to poor, young to old, was given unmeasured amounts of booze.

When some Jatts started shaking under the influence, the venue was filled with requests for raunchy Punjabi songs. Anwarjan was happy to oblige. While singing, she became a bartender. Everyone jostled with each other to experience the heavenly pleasure of receiving a drink poured from her hand.

Pala Singh was used to drinking heavily, but Bhai Dasondha Singh had never been fortunate enough to have an unlimited supply of alcohol like this. So, he took advantage of the situation and filled his belly.

For Karam Chand and the pandit, it was the best day of their life. Anwarjan was simply handing drinks to the others, but for them, she was touching the glasses to their lips until they gulped down every drop. When she moved a step further by taking a sip from the glasses before serving them, it almost killed them both.

The milieu had changed dramatically from the start of the evening. The guests were in another world. Some swayed with their eyes closed, others sang Anwarjan's praises, but most were gone too far to do even that.

Anwarjan gestured to the orchestra to wind up the show. They had worked longer than usual and been showered with enough money. They packed up their instruments and headed towards their rooms. The guests started to disperse as well. But those who were too drunk to move remained there.

28

A CRESTFALLEN BACHAN SINGH showed up at Sundri's house around 8 p.m. Worried about him, she held his hand and asked, 'What happened? Is everything fine?'

He sat on the bed and sighed heavily. 'Sundri, I've failed,' he said and told her everything that had happened at Diwanpur.

Sundri was upset. They had both pledged themselves to a mission of reform, but it was Bachan Singh alone who was bearing this burden.

She thought for a while. Suddenly, her face lit up. 'Now it's my turn,' she said.

'Your turn? How can you succeed when I've not been able to despite trying for days?'

Sundri looked at him with determination. 'It doesn't matter if I'm successful, but I must try my best. Of course, everything is in the Almighty's hands.'

'No, Sundri, no, I don't want you to be in danger.'

'Just listen to me; I've thought of a plan.'

'What is it?'

'Instead of bothering with the branches, why don't we deal with the root itself?'

'What do you mean?'

'Why don't we talk to the dancer?'

Bachan Singh burst into laughter. 'Oh, Sundri! That isn't going to help. You cannot tame a lion like an ordinary pet.'

'I want to give it a try if you'll allow me.'

'All right, if you've made up your mind, I won't dissuade you. But I still think it's going to be futile.'

'Whatever it is…'

'Fine, as you wish.'

'Please accompany me to Diwanpur so that I can try.'

'How will you come back from there at midnight?'

'I won't need to. I can stay for the rest of the night at your place.'

'All right, let's go', said Bachan Singh, and they left for Diwanpur.

29

IT WAS 10 P.M. A big crowd lingered around Anwarjan's place, but she finally got rid of them, saying she had a headache. Her maid closed the door and made her bed.

Anwarjan had just fallen asleep when there was a knock at the door. She woke up with irritation. 'These rascals won't let me rest, even after I kicked them out with so much difficulty', she muttered to herself and sent her maid to open the door.

Hearing the sound of steps, she got up and saw a beautiful girl of sixteen or seventeen following the maid. 'Come here, *beti,*' Anwarjan said gently, 'what brings you here at this hour of the night?'

It was the first time in her life that a woman had called Sundri '*beti*'. As a child, whenever she had heard mothers calling their daughters '*bacchi*', '*beti*', '*puttar*', or other terms of endearment, she had been filled with an intense yearning for the love of a mother. She had always longed to hear this small word, and the moment Anwarjan uttered it, all hateful thoughts vanished from Sundri's mind.

On her way there, Sundri had wondered how she would face such a disgraceful woman. Everything in her room would be tainted with sin; how would she touch anything? And though she had earlier imagined talking to Anwarjan from a distance, Sundri was now unwittingly drawn towards her.

Anwarjan's maid left, and Sundri stood still near her bed. 'Can I help you, *beti*?' Anwarjan asked again.

She bowed her head. 'Yes, Ma ji. You can help me.'

Anwarjan was touched by the way Sundri addressed her. She held Sundri's hand and helped her sit on the bed. 'Yes, *beti*?'

Sundri looked into Anwarjan's eyes and said, 'Ma ji! I've come to make a humble request of you, but…'

She paused. Anwarjan gazed into Sundri's eyes but could not guess what the girl wanted to say. She put her arm around Sundri's shoulder and pulled her close. 'Tell me, my child, why are you keeping quiet?'

A strange warmth blossomed inside Sundri at Anwarjan's touch, even though she had thought of the woman as perverse just a few minutes ago. She took Anwarjan's other hand into both of hers. 'Ma ji, this is difficult for me, I don't feel like I can say anything to you.'

Anwarjan released her hand gently and wrapped her arm around Sundri's waist. 'No, my child', she said, 'Why are you feeling shy? I'll do whatever you ask me.' But as soon she had uttered those words, she realized she had perhaps spoken too hastily. She should not have made a promise before hearing what Sundri had to say.

Sundri still clung to Anwarjan. 'Ma ji…!' she said but

could not utter anything more. Her heart filled up every time she spoke those words. Love surged through her veins. She was like a person inhaling the sweet fragrance of a flower. She felt like repeating the words over and over. 'Ma ji!' she said again.

Anwarjan did not hear her. She had started to comb Sundri's hair with her fingers. She had forgotten that Sundri was asking something of her. She felt peace in Sundri's presence, the glow of a maternal love she had always longed for.

Sundri rested her head on Anwarjan's chest and looked up at her.

Anwarjan noticed tears in Sundri's eyes. She pulled out a handkerchief from underneath the pillow and wiped her face, and then tenderly kissed her on the forehead.

Sundri threw her arms around Anwarjan's neck.

'*Beti*!' Anwarjan said, 'Tell me what you wanted to speak about. I'll do whatever I can for you.'

Recognising the sincerity in Anwarjan's words, Sundri spoke up. 'Ma ji, don't you hate your profession?'

Anwarjan looked searchingly at Sundri's face. 'Of course. I hate this profession as much as you do.'

'Then why don't you leave it, Ma ji?'

'Because there's nowhere else for me in this world.'

'What do you mean?'

'You cannot understand this, my child.'

'Why, Ma ji?'

'You're still unmarried, aren't you?'

'Yes.' Sundri said, looking down.

'That's why you cannot understand my wretched condition and the circumstances that led me here. Any woman who becomes a widow on the first day of marriage, whose in-laws throw her out like a fly in milk, into a world of criminals and monsters, can understand my condition.'

Hatred flashed across Anwarjan's face. The veins on her forehead throbbed, and her eyes became red.

Sundri felt as if a hungry lion had been unleashed before her. Her heartbeat quickened. She felt scared and thought of running away.

Anwarjan continued in fury. 'In a world where fraud, dishonesty, selfishness and wickedness prevail, where someone like me has to become a woman of the streets to survive, where demons in the garb of father or brother conspire to assault a helpless woman, where an infant is snatched mercilessly from a mother and thrown before crows and dogs... what else can a woman do except adopt such a profession in a world like this? I just told you I hate this profession... but no, that's not true. I don't hate it. Why would I hate a profession that draws rich and influential people to my doorstep? I consider it a miracle, a blessing. It has provided me with everything – respect, wealth and reputation. The only thing it has deprived me of is my daughter, who was taken away from me by a cruel monster. A wildfire of revenge burns inside me... I want to kill them, burn all of them to ashes...' While speaking, Anwarjan started howling as if her body was about to explode. She threw herself on the pillow and started sobbing.

Sundri panicked. She felt her head reeling, fear coursing through her. She fled down the stairs without speaking or listening to anything else, leaving Anwarjan behind.

Before she could exit the house, however, she stopped abruptly. She found herself going back to Anwarjan's room. Why was she returning? She could not explain it.

The door to the stairs was still open. She stepped inside, and bumped into someone in the dark. Startled, she embraced the unseen person like a sleeping child embraces its mother tightly out of fear.

After Sundri left, Anwarjan, still crying, got up from her bed and looked around the room. She was shocked to find Sundri missing and ran downstairs. In the dark, she bumped into someone, someone who was now clinging to her.

Both of them went back upstairs to the same room. Sundri lay her head in Anwarjan's lap. After a while, Anwarjan looked into Sundri's eyes. 'What's your name, my child?' she asked.

'Sundri.'

'Sundri! I do not know why I am so drawn to you. Had you not met me at the door, I would have gone after you. Where do you live? Who is your father?'

'He is no more.'

'What was his profession?'

'He was a juggler.'

'He earned his living by entertaining people?'

'Yes.'

Anwarjan looked at Sundri's face intently and thought to

herself, *such a beauty at a juggler's house!*

'And, what about your mother?'

'I don't have a mother.'

'Oh! My poor child. When did your mother die?'

'I don't know.'

'You don't know?'

'I never had a mother.'

Anwarjan smiled at Sundri's answer. 'Did she die while you were very young?'

'No.'

'Then?'

'She never existed.'

'Then how were you born?'

'I wasn't born…' Sundri said hastily but immediately realized how silly she sounded. 'I mean, my baba found me under a bush.'

Noticing the odd expressions on Anwarjan's face, she suddenly felt like she was intruding, that she was interrupting the woman's sleep. She stood up. 'All right, Ma ji, I'll take your leave. I've already taken enough of your time. I'll meet you another day.'

Anwarjan held Sundri's arm before she could leave and made her sit down again. 'My child, what village did he bring you from?'

'Near his own cottage on the outskirts of this village.'

Sundri told Anwarjan all about her life until that day, about Rodu's hut, about how she had grown up. Anwarjan cried uncontrollably as she listened.

Perhaps she has lost someone close to her, Sundri thought. *Perhaps she's remembering them*. She hugged Anwarjan and asked gently, 'Ma ji, why are you crying?'

Anwarjan held Sundri tightly. She seemed weak after sobbing. She wanted to speak, but the words did not leave her lips. Finally, with great difficulty, she said, 'My sweet unfortunate girl. I am your own mother from whom you were snatched and thrown into the jungle.'

Sundri almost collapsed with the shock of what she heard. A wave of emotions passed through Sundri as she clung to Anwarjan. 'Ma ji', she said, 'You... you...'

But Anwarjan did not respond. She got up abruptly with a jerk, as if struck by a sudden thought, and separated herself from Sundri. She took a step backwards. 'Oh, my child! You should not touch my polluted body. You are the child of a sinful mother; you must hate me. My innocent angel! This place is full of filth; you shouldn't be here. Be quick and...' She covered her face with her hands as she spoke, shrinking in on herself as if trying to vanish from the room. The love that had filled her just a few moments ago had now turned into shame. The thought that her daughter knew of her profession was excruciating to her. She ran like a madwoman to a corner of the room and started crying again.

Sundri was stunned. Everything seemed like a dream. Anwarjan's voice echoed through the room again. She was mumbling like a lunatic.

Now, she was extending her hands towards Sundri, still sobbing. 'No, no, my child! I am innocent. When I tell you about the person responsible for my ruin, maybe you will not think so poorly of me.'

Sundri felt as if someone was stabbing her with a knife, carving out pieces of her flesh. She ran towards Anwarjan and grabbed her. 'Ma ji, I do not doubt your innocence, but you must tell me what led you to such a state.'

Anwarjan managed to position herself on the bed and told Sundri everything, from the beginning until the day she had been forced to abandon her own baby in the jungle.

A blind rage, like a fire, swept over Sundri as she listened. The same society that had shunned her and treated her with scorn, which had tortured both the man she loved and the man who had been a father to her, that same society was also responsible for the plight of her mother. Flames of revenge lapped her insides. Bachan Singh's ideals and teachings vanished from her mind. She found it difficult to remain seated. Her body began to tremble. But there was a lot more left to understand. Trying to control her emotions, she asked, 'Then what happened, Ma ji?'

'My child, I'm not strong enough to express my love for you. You were left under the open sky to be devoured by eagles and crows. When Tara Chand, your cruel father, deserted me while I was sick and pregnant, I was left with no money, nothing except some kitchen utensils. He had already robbed me of everything before leaving the house.'

Sundri noticed that a cold, deadly expression appeared on Anwarjan's face when she talked about Tara Chand. She was gasping for breath now. At one point, she even forgot what she was saying and had to drink a glass of water to steel herself. She continued, 'It was around 2 p.m. when you decided to enter the world. I had nowhere to go, but two Muslim women entered my house through the roof. Perhaps they heard the cries of a newborn child. May God bless them! They took care of everything. I did not want to live, and yet I was alive. One of them was a nurse who looked after me through the night.

'The next day, the women gathered some men from their community in the neighbourhood. They informed a Hindu man about the incident and brought him to me. One of the Muslims, whose wife had saved my life, said that he and his family had been taking care of me since last night. He said his wife had given me water and fed me hot milk to keep me alive.

'The Hindu man was shocked to hear this. He touched his ears and ran from there, saying I could not enter their premises now that my religion had been defiled since I had eaten and drank from the hands of Muslims.

'The Muslims were stunned and regretted being as honest as they had been. I was better by then. I was used to such treatment from Hindu society; Choudhry's cruelty only made my heart grow stronger. I asked my saviours if I could stay with them for ten days since my own community refused to provide me shelter.

'One of them said, "Sister! You can stay with us for ten years if you wish. We would happily provide for you just as we're providing for our own daughters and sisters. But we are worried about the objections your community will raise to you staying here".'

'I was enraged. "The same Hindu society that turned me out on the streets? That ruined me for no offence? That reduced my life to ashes? Do you consider such a society as human? I have nothing but hatred for such a society and will continue to do so until I'm dead. If you have some compassion in your hearts, please let me stay for a few days."

'Then another one of them said, "You're as good as our own sister. We will do our best to keep you safe and happy, but we're simple labourers, we don't have much money, and we won't be able to arrange a separate cook to make your meals." "I don't need any cook," I told them. "I'll eat whatever you prepare yourselves."

'I spent nearly two weeks at their home, and they gave me extraordinary care and attention. On the fifteenth day after your birth, Choudhry visited me again. "Bibi!" he said with great tenderness, "I've been worried about you since I first came to see you. I've arranged for you to live at a home for widows in Delhi. You'll be provided with all the comforts and an education there."

'I remembered his reluctance to help me just two weeks ago, and so I did not agree immediately. But my Muslim brothers thought it would be a good idea, and I finally made up my mind to leave for Delhi.

'He came the next day and took me to the railway station. By now, his sweet and comforting words had won my trust.

We were on the train, speeding along. I was resting on the window seat and he was sitting opposite, telling me all about the ashram and the arrangements there. But all of a sudden, his face became serious. "Oh! But I've forgotten to tell you something," he said.

"What?" I asked him.

"They have a rule barring anyone from bringing a child with them to the ashram."

'My sweet child, I was feeding you at that time. I remember looking down at your innocent face with enormous love.' "What!" I asked him in disbelief.

'He told me he had a relative in the town at the next station. "If you don't mind, we can hand over the baby to him," he said. "And after some time, when she's more grown up, we'll get her back."

'I was filled with fear when I heard him. How can a mother leave her newborn child with a stranger? My heart was sinking. But he was clever and wicked and managed to convince me that it was the right thing to do. We got off at the next station. He hired a tonga and took me to a nearby village called Diwanpur – I only came to know what it was called later.

'He made me wait with you under a tree, saying he would go meet his relative. He returned after a while and said, "I've arranged with my relatives to take care of your child. But it would be inappropriate to bring you before them. Just trust me and do what I say. Leave the child next to that big bush near the cottage. They'll collect him from there." I was in a trance, completely naïve, and even though my heart was telling me not to, I eventually did what he asked me to. It was only later that I found out he was a fraud and had fooled me. He had not arranged anything at all.

'When we reached Delhi, we went to a posh house. The drawing room was well-decorated, filled with expensive furniture. No one was in the house. He told me that it belonged to a friend of his.

'He asked a maid to look after me and left saying that he would come back in the morning and accompany me to the home for widows.

'Though that house had all the comforts of the world, I couldn't sleep for a single moment that night. I remained worried about you. The maid took good care of me, but I couldn't stop myself from weeping.

'In the morning, after I had bathed and changed, an old madam came to me. Before I could speak, she asked me, "*Beti*, are you comfortable here? I had to be away last night, but this old maid is quite dependable. I hope she provided you with everything you needed."

'I was stunned. I looked at her from head to toe, and asked, "Is this house yours?"

"Yes, my child, by God's grace."

'I asked her, "Where is Choudhry?"

'She said, "Which Choudhry?"

'I said, "The person who brought me here so I can join the ashram for widows."

'She laughed. '*Beti*! Who can keep count of the Choudhrys and Khans? Hundreds of them come and go here. But I understand. You're asking about the man who has sold you to me. He left last night after keeping the promise he had made you. This is the *real* home for widows, where thousands of women are looked after as they enjoy a life of luxury."

'The woman's words shocked me to my core, but what could I do? I shouted and cried; I refused food and water for days, but it did not make any difference to the old woman. She tried her best to keep me under control; she kept insisting that I would have a rich and spectacular life. But when her words did not work, she deputed a young woman to do the job. In the end, she succeeded in convincing me to join this disgusting profession. I don't think I would have agreed, but when that young woman told me she belonged to a well-off Brahmin family and how the torments inflicted by her own community had forced her to adopt this line of work, my heart melted. And I shed my dignity forever.

'Later, I told her my story. Even as she listened, infuriated, she insisted everything that had happened to me further proved her point. "Why are you so concerned about those who trampled you under their feet for no fault of yours? Now it's our turn to expose the rotten truth of this supposedly moralistic society..."

'From that day on, I shunned my community and my religion. I killed off the little self-respect that remained in my life. From Gurdei, I became Anwarjan. I started learning the art of dancing, singing and entertaining. I was already blessed with an attractive figure, sharp features and a fair complexion. And in just a few weeks, I became immensely popular.

'When I was an upright Hindu woman, I was insulted, tormented and thrown aside like a dead rodent. But today, despite being a Muslim woman and an entertainer, the leaders of my community, the so-called *keepers* of religion and culture, visit me and feel privileged to lick the soles of my shoes. This filthy and rotten slice of society, so foul that worms crawl everywhere in it, whose revolting odour would make even a healthy person sick, now bestows honours upon me.

'Do you know what this pomp and show is about, my child? It's my stepson's wedding. Had you come half an hour earlier, you would have seen a fascinating drama unfold. Karam Chand, the groom's brother and my eldest stepson, who kicked me out of his house after beating me, came here along with that wicked pandit. Would you like to know why they had come? Karam Chand had come to beg for my love with head bent over the feet of a woman of the street. And that old rascal, the pandit, who had once called me "*beti*", that abominable sinner who sold me to your father Tara Chand, also came here to beg for my attention, for my love. Sundri, had you heard their words of longing and desire, had you listened to a son begging for that kind of adoration from a mother; and a father from a daughter, I'm sure you would have wished for the earth to swallow you on the spot. Those rats wouldn't have left me alone all night if I hadn't made an excuse and put them off till tomorrow.

'Do you want to know why I'm here? It is not to entertain

these sinners. I only agreed to come here because my heart burns with revenge. Sundri! I've come here to kill them both. I have been waiting for this wedding for a long time. I even hired four men for the job. I've already got rid of the third one, the one who sold me to that old woman, and nobody has been able to trace it to me. I don't want to disturb you by telling you the details of that murder. But I yearn to finish off these men and that butcher Tara Chand. I've been trying to find him but haven't been successful. Yet. When I track him down...'

Sundri could not bear to hear anything more. Her whole body was burning like charcoal. Although Bachan Singh's teachings had helped temper her violent thoughts to some extent, all thoughts of goodness had now vanished, like a sapling uprooted by a strong gust of wind. She felt the earth slipping from under her feet and everything spinning before her eyes. She got up and shouted, 'I'll kill that bastard, Ma ji. I am making this pledge before you. I'll start looking for him immediately...'

Engulfed by the clouds of a deadly passion, she ran downstairs.

Anwarjan remained seated even after Sundri had left, still as a statue. Her own words rang in her ears. Everything that had happened that day seemed like a dream to her.

It was past midnight when Sundri came out from Anwarjan's house. She found Bachan Singh waiting for her in the street, and they both left for his house.

30

BACK HOME, BACHAN SINGH looked at Sundri's face carefully in the light of the lamp. Her eyes were ablaze with a savage fire. There was a violent smile on her face.

He shook her shoulder. 'What's the matter, Sundri?'

'Nothing! Everything is fine.' Aware of Bachan Singh watching her, Sundri tried to quell the turbulence inside her. 'Did you go to the wedding venue again?' she asked, trying to divert his attention.

'No, I stayed home.' Bachan Singh said, before asking again, 'Sundri, your eyes are red. What's wrong?'

She rubbed her eyes, pretending she was just tired from a lack of sleep. 'It is the result of your blessing only.'

'Why?'

'Because of the responsibility you assigned to me.'

'Tell me how it went?'

'Everything went well.'

'You were successful?'

'Entirely successful.'

'Impossible.'

'More than possible!'

'What do you mean?'

Sundri told him Anwarjan had promised to quit her profession forever.

Bachan Singh looked at her, unconvinced. 'Sundri, it seems like she has swayed you with a false promise.'

Sundri's face had a firm expression. 'Whatever it might be', she said, 'I'm sure she'll never dance in public again. You'll come to know about it.'

'If this is true, I'd say you've managed to extract oil from sand. Let's say Anwarjan doesn't perform tomorrow; the *baraat* will leave the day after tomorrow. So you made her promise not to perform at all while she's in Diwanpur?'

Sundri had a little smile on her lips. 'A bit more than that.'

'What?'

'Yesterday's performance was the last performance of her life.'

'How can this be possible, Sundri?' He looked into her eyes. 'How is it possible to make a vulture give up the practice of eating dead flesh forever…'

Sundri convinced him about Anwarjan's retirement but did not tell him what else had happened that day. She knew that if he found out the pledge she had taken before her mother, he would force her to break it.

Bachan Singh was unable to control his excitement. 'Sundri!' he shouted with joy, 'we'll definitely be successful now.'

'No, we're already successful.'

'Sundri! When will we become one from two?'

'We're already one.'

'We're certainly one on the divine front, but not in the eyes of society.'

Sundri took Bachan Singh's hand into hers. 'What society are you talking about? The one riddled with suspicion, jealousy, contempt, malice? If this society cannot already see us as one, it is the fault of their own vision. You might think of them as human beings, but I know...'

Bitterness and hatred overpowered Sundri. Her face glowed red like an ember, and her heart beat faster.

The sudden transformation on Sundri's face alarmed Bachan Singh. He looked into her eyes. She appeared to have gone mad.

Some ailments are difficult to cure. Expert treatment by a capable doctor can bring relief to the patient to some extent, but all it takes is a little carelessness by the patient to cause the illness to flare again. Such was Sundri's condition. Bachan Singh had tirelessly guided her to the right path but had not been successful completely, and the recent encounter with Anwarjan had given fresh life to all her old destructive thoughts.

'What's wrong with you today, Sundri?' Bachan Singh asked, holding her arm. And yet, in the next moment, he was worried that continuing the discussion would only aggravate the violence that seemed to be raging inside Sundri. 'Anyway, let's forget about this for now,' he continued, 'We must plan further. What do you say?'

Sundri had controlled her emotions with great effort but regretted her outburst. Bachan Singh could not know. She spoke in a rush, grateful for the change in subject. 'But you wrote in your last letter that you aren't able to travel much...

'Yes, but we must continue our mission. The success of our first effort has encouraged me tremendously. The task that I couldn't complete even after several weeks of struggle... you have accomplished in the first attempt. That's why I suggest we must get...'

Sundri interrupted, 'I have done nothing. It's all your companionship and teachings otherwise, what can be expected from a monkey-girl like me? What do you wish to do now?'

'We should get married so that we can move freely together to fulfil our mission.'

Sundri smiled shyly. 'But can't we do that without getting married?'

'No, that is impossible.'

'I don't consider it impossible.'

'Then let me know your thoughts.'

'We must work apart from each other for some time, and after finishing our respective tasks, become one until the end of this universe.'

'Sundri, I don't understand what you're saying. Your words are scaring me.'

'Do you think there is room for fear in the path of love? For the first time, I've heard an unreasonable statement from you. All I mean to say is...' but Sundri fell silent.

Gripped by panic, Bachan Singh asked, 'Yes, what do you mean?'

'What I mean to say is for you to… to forget me for some time.'

'Forget you?' Bachan Singh said in agony. 'What are you saying? You said no such thing before going to Anwarjan's house.'

'Yes! Forget about me,' Sundri continued, paying no heed to his words. 'And if you cannot forget me, then keep my memory in your heart forever.'

Bachan Singh's eyes glistened. He held Sundri's hand tenderly. 'For God's sake, don't talk like this. Take pity on me.'

Sundri held Bachan Singh's hand tightly in hers. Suppressing her own emotions, she said, 'Why are you talking like this? I'm yours, only yours, forever yours. Please don't break the barrier of my patience and the strength of my pledge.'

It was as if Sundri was trying to extinguish the fire in Bachan Singh's heart, the incredible thirst he felt, by pouring yet more fire onto it.

'Sundri!' he said, 'Please don't speak in riddles. Tell me everything clearly.'

Sundri attempted a laugh. 'I'll speak clearly. I am aware of all the problems you've faced for me. Had they come to an end, I would have been able to tolerate it, but I can now see that you will have to suffer even more because of my existence. I wish you to leave me alone for some time. Take care of your mother while she's alive and fulfil her cherished dream of getting you married. She'll forget all these worries when she has a daughter-in-law at home.'

Bachan Singh felt like his chest was being pierced with a volley of sharp arrows. He covered his face with one hand and gestured at Sundri with the other, asking her to stop speaking. 'Sundri! For heaven's sake, stop this. Marrying anyone else but you will be death for me. I cannot hear any more of this.'

Sundri did not pay attention to his words. Her thoughts were somewhere else. Bachan Singh stood up to leave. He decided it was best to speak to her later when it would be possible to clear her mind of these strange notions.

The light of dawn was dispelling the darkness of the night. When Bachan Singh started walking towards his room, Sundri looked at him with a distant smile. 'Are you leaving?' she asked.

'Yes, I will clear these misgivings of yours later.'

'I wish these were just misgivings…'

After Bachan Singh left, Sundri lay down. Her sleepless eyes filled with images of Anwarjan.

31

AFTER STAYING AWAKE FOR most of the night, Sundri's eyes were finally filled with sleep by a cool breeze, but it was full of dread and fearful dreams. She seemed to have been thrown into a world where everything – earth, sky, moon, sun – was full of blood. Her eyes and ears were being pierced with sharp weapons. Every pore of the earth was bleeding. The birds, perched on the trees, were terrified. The water in the rivers, wells, and ponds had turned to blood. Wherever she went, she heard sounds of death. Blood was dripping from her clothes, her hair, her eyes and her mouth. She was drowning in a river of blood. Every creature in it, from the smallest fish to the biggest and fattest crocodile, oozed blood. They seemed to have human tongues, and as they chased each other, they screamed for violence. Every being, cruel, powerful, or weak, had just one word to say, 'blood.'

Sundri felt herself sinking into the riverbed. She could not breathe properly. She tried to shout for help, but the cry did not leave her lips and was lost inside her. She turned abruptly on her side and found her arms crossed over her chest. The sunrays filled her room, but even the walls seemed covered in blood instead of the warm yellow light. Shouts of 'murder!, murder!' rang in her ears.

She immediately closed her eyes again in fear. The voices were still tearing at her eardrums. She opened her eyes again and got up from her bed. The sun had risen high. She felt the entire house surrounded by the noise. The shouts were coming from everywhere.

She came out of the house to find the whole village gathered around Bachan Singh. The police had handcuffed him. His mother was sobbing uncontrollably. Someone shouted from the crowd, 'Bachan Singh has killed three people – a street dancer, an old pandit and Karam Chand.'

A cloud of darkness engulfed Sundri. She rushed out of the house and forced her way through the crowd. As she clung to Bachan Singh, a loud cry escaped her body, and she fell unconscious at his feet. The crowd continued moving.

Everything appeared as a dream to Bachan Singh, but his heart sank when he saw Sundri fall. He looked back several times and even tried to stop to help her, but the constables pushed him further toward the police station.

Meanwhile, the news that Bachan Singh had killed three people in one night spread like wildfire through the village.

When Sundri regained consciousness, she found herself covered in dust, lying in her old house in Rawani. Some of the villagers had brought her there.

Sundri's head was reeling. She felt as if a bomb had gone off in her head, taking away her ability to think. She felt everything go dark around her and fainted again.

She remained in that state for a long time. When she regained consciousness for the second time, she wondered if she had heard the news of Bachan Singh's arrest in her dream.

She got up and staggered towards the road to Diwanpur. Several people tried to stop her, but she kept walking until finally, she spotted a tonga on the road and got into it.

When she reached Diwanpur, she found Bachan Singh's mother lying in bed, surrounded by women from the neighbourhood, trying to bring her back to her senses. Sundri looked around at everyone as if crazed but did not speak to anyone, nor did anyone call upon her.

When Bachan Singh's mother opened her eyes, Sundri rushed towards her. But when she saw Sundri, Sada Kaur's face turned crimson with rage. She jerked away from Sundri. 'Why are you here, you filthy bitch! Get lost! All hell has broken loose in this house because of you. Ever since you showed your wretched face to my son, there has been only chaos in his life. Go! May you be ruined forever!' Overwhelmed by her outburst, she started sobbing.

Had anyone else said such words to Sundri, she would have reacted with the same viciousness. Instead, she listened quietly, like a lion who does not accept a challenge from anyone in the jungle but, when caged in a zoo, is completely helpless.

Sundri rushed to the police station instead. On the way, the enormity of what was happening struck her like a wound that does not hurt as much when fresh but becomes intolerably painful after some time. She was like a deer, facing a hunter with a shotgun in front, a jungle on fire at its back, a big river on its right, and a cruel settlement of human beings on its left.

She trembled. Her lover, more important to her than all the treasures of the world, was trapped in a case of triple murder. His mother was nothing without him. The women surrounding her at the moment with false sympathy were good for nothing. And the entire village, already hostile towards Bachan Singh, would not hesitate to paint him as a killer.

Sundri felt like she was in a boat without a rudder. Her father Rodu had been killed by those cold-blooded murderers. She had found her mother, but she had sparkled just once like lightning in a black sky and then vanished forever. Sundri knew she would not be allowed to stay in Rawani because the entire village was afraid of Pala Singh and his men. Where could she go, especially when Bachan Singh was trapped? The people of Diwanpur already scorned her.

For the first time in her life, she realized how weak and helpless a woman is in the world.

Sundri kept walking while lost in these thoughts, making plans and then discarding them, unable to reach a resolution. She was most worried about not being able to help Bachan Singh. She felt like ending her life before facing yet another blow. At least she would get rid of all her troubles that way. But some hidden power within her did not let her take such a drastic step. Over and over, she thought: *Had my mother left a suicide note before killing her enemies and herself, this would not have happened.*

When she arrived at the police station, she was denied permission to meet Bachan Singh but was, instead, chased away by the guards.

Throughout the day, Sundri struggled to meet the heads of the village, begging them to arrange a meeting with Bachan Singh, but no one paid heed to her. Wherever she went, she received jeers and taunts.

At last, sobbing, Sundri returned to Rawani by dusk and fell into her bed.

She spent the next day like a bird with broken wings fallen to the ground – miserable and helpless. She lay in bed without eating or drinking. No one came to speak with her, nor did she want them to.

Early in the morning on the following day, there was a knock at her door. It was a police constable, with whom Bachan Singh had sent a letter for her. He handed it over to her and left immediately. Sundri came back inside and started reading:

Sundri!

Something that couldn't be imagined even in a dream has happened. I can well imagine your state of mind after my arrest. How painful it is! My heart is burning like a furnace.

Sundri, I wish I could bring happiness into your life at

least once. But I'm unfortunate to not be blessed with such a privilege.

My heavenly goddess, my heart tells me that soon we will be separated forever. A voice inside me is saying we were destined to be together for the limited time we've already spent. This accusation against me is not ordinary; I do not anticipate an acquittal based on everything I've heard about how the villagers are presenting this case.

But Sundri, do you, too, doubt my innocence? Does your heart say I'm a murderer? I don't care if the whole world considers me so or even if the court hangs me to death. But Sundri! If you, too, think the same of me, I will not be able to bear it.

I don't have the time to write more. I've managed to send this message to you with great difficulty. The same constable will come to you again. Send your response cautiously through him; he is worried about his honour and job.

I'm writing to Giani ji as well. He is staying at the gurdwara these days. He will come and take you away. It's no longer safe for you to remain in Diwanpur.

Sundri, if you want to remain in peace, please don't even think of coming to me. I'll somehow manage to exchange letters. Consider them as meetings. Can you imagine my condition if I were to see you? I'll be dead even before death comes to me.

With every chime of the jail clock, I feel a new problem is arising for me. How should I explain my state of mind to you? I'm trying my best to console you, but there's no one here to console me. But whatsoever is destined will happen now.

Sundri, even as I advise you to stay away, I wish I could talk to you in person. All my worries and tensions appear to have escaped me in this moment of communicating with you.

Yours,
Bachan Singh

An array of expressions flashed across Sundri's face as she read the letter. But in the end, there was a hot glow on her face. Every pore of her being was filled with courage.

She got up instantly, took out her pen and paper and started writing:

My master,

I have read your letter. You've accepted defeat so easily, despite being a righteous and innocent man! Why?

My love! If this cruel and selfish world considers me worth less than a fake coin, then I think of it as less than a fourth of that. What did you say; you couldn't bring happiness in my life? You're wrong!

When I had written those letters to you in the past, I was unaware of the path of love, but now, not only do I understand its importance and purity, but it has become indispensable in my life. All those words I wrote you now seem shallow, devoid of experience.

My master! Earlier, I was in love only with your physical existence, but now that I am in love with your soul, I am safe. I know no power can take me away from you.

What worries you, my love? Death? It may be known as 'death' in this world's limited vocabulary, but it is, in fact, a final destination. It appears you don't value this destination or are perhaps unaware of it. My master, this final destination is where we will become a single entity, where the world's rotten eyes, infected with jealousy, will not interfere in our love. It is where we will be honoured on the sacred throne and sitting together in each other's embrace, even Brahma will not be able to separate us. Do you still call it 'death'? It is blatantly untrue and unfair.

Does your heart really believe we are going to be separated forever? No, my love, no.

Your truthfulness... how can I ever doubt it? Not only do I know you are innocent, but I also know who the real killer is. But whom do I tell this? Who will believe me?

I'm sure Anwarjan committed suicide after killing those two men. Perhaps she asked them to visit after I left that night and then killed them on the spot. But I do not know how to present this truth before the court.

You have called Giani ji for my safety; this is good, but going with him and leaving you in the clutches of death is impossible for me. Can I do nothing to save your life? I know someone like me is worth nothing, but how can I abandon the mission of reform you started? I still have the power of my pen.

But my master! I never knew that you could be so weak of heart. Be strong, and do not let fear come near you. I've been trying hard since yesterday to meet you. Though you have asked me to avoid it, forgive me for needing to fulfil this desire.

You are advising me to be brave, my love. I wish you to follow this advice yourself. If you want to make me happy, I must see you in high spirits, with renewed confidence.

Merged with you forever,
Yours Sundri

32

EVER SINCE BACHAN SINGH'S arrest, Sundri had stopped teaching. She no longer cared about eating or changing her clothes. From morning to evening, she visited lawyers and police officers or went chasing after witnesses and made pleas before them. But despite all her efforts, she had gotten nowhere. Even as the court had recorded statements from Bachan Singh's mother, her relatives were already trying to claim her assets.

Pala Singh, meanwhile, was looking for an opportunity to grab hold of Sundri. The major obstacle in his path had been removed. He had played the game with such expertise that there was little hope left for Bachan Singh's survival.

Bachan Singh was charged under Section 302 of the Indian Penal Code. Lala Rala Ram and his son had given their statements: 'Bachan Singh had threatened us with dire consequences if Anwarjan's performance was not cancelled, but when we refused, he warned us that he would handle us "in another way".'

Pala Singh had given a statement as well: 'Bachan Singh met me one day before the incident and said, "I want you to provide me someone who can kill three people. I'll pay one hundred and fifty rupees." But when I refused, he said he'll manage everything on his own.'

One of Pala Singh's men said, 'I saw Bachan Singh with a knife near Anwarjan's house that night.' Another one said, 'I saw him early morning at the village well, washing his blood-stained clothes.' Someone else said, 'On the night of the crime, I saw him climbing the stairs of Anwarjan's house. Karam Chand and Pandit ji were already there to discuss something regarding her dance performance.'

Then, a blacksmith, after seeing the blood-stained knife recovered from Anwarjan's room, said, 'This knife was made at my shop, and Bachan Singh bought it from me.'

For her part, Sundri decided to mention everything about her meeting with Anwarjan to the lawyer hired by Bachan Singh's mother. But she thought it was crucial to speak to Bachan Singh first.

And after struggling for days, Sundri could finally meet Bachan Singh.

33

BACHAN SINGH WAS LODGED inside a small, dingy cell at the jailhouse. The same constable, who had carried the letters between Sundri and Bachan Singh, had arranged their meeting.

It was 5 p.m. The prisoners who had visitors coming that day were brought from their cells into a verandah adjoining the jail corridor. Bachan Singh was among them.

As Bachan Singh looked anxiously through the metal grill wrapped around the verandah, he finally spotted Sundri coming towards him. He held his breath. Sundri was in a bad state. Her skin was incredibly pale as if there was no blood left in her body, her clothes were dirty, and her hair was dishevelled. She looked like a walking corpse. She walked through the jail with a dejected stagger. It seemed as if she would fall any moment.

When she neared him, Bachan Singh extended his hand through the grill and shook her by the arm. 'Sundri! Where has your courage gone? You asked me to be brave, but look at your own condition…' But Sundri did not understand what Bachan Singh was saying. Since the last few days, she had been determined to remain strong and had not shed a tear.

But the moment she came before Bachan Singh, the dam broke. Her body shook with sobs; she seemed inconsolable.

'Sundri! We don't have much time,' Bachan Singh said. Realizing her state, Sundri wiped her eyes.

Bachan Singh cleared his throat. 'Sundri, this is why I asked you to avoid meeting me.'

'But how could I not?' Sundri said with a gasp. 'I had to meet you to let you know something important.'

'What is it?'

'I've cheated you by not telling you the truth.'

'What do you mean?'

Sundri told him everything about her meeting with Anwarjan, everything she had concealed from him about that day.

Bachan Singh was stunned. He had been under the impression that it was Pala Singh who had hatched the plan to trap him, and either he or one of his men had committed the murders. But it hadn't all added up. If Pala Singh wanted to implicate him in the murder case and steal Anwarjan's money and jewellery, then why had he killed Karam Chand and Pandit Radhey Krishan? He had assumed the two men arrived at the scene and Pala Singh killed them to eliminate any witnesses.

But as he heard the truth from Sundri, Bachan Singh started trembling. For a while, he could not utter a word. The thought of how Sundri's mother's life had come to an end horrified him.

He now knows I'm the daughter of a cheap street dancer, Sundri thought, unable to look into Bachan Singh's eyes.

Bachan Singh knew the heaviness that must lay on Sundri and decided not to say anything else at that moment. 'It is all so strange, Sundri', he said instead. 'Oh, hasn't Giani ji come yet?'

'No, he should reach this evening.'

'Will you go with him?'

'No, I can't go yet.'

'Why not?'

'I need to have my statement recorded in court.'

'What statement?'

'Everything that I've just told you. I need to prove your innocence.'

Bachan Singh smiled. 'Sundri, who will believe you? Maybe if Anwarjan had left a note taking responsibility for the murders, there could have been a chance of my survival. But now it'll be nothing but entertainment for the villagers.'

'I do not care if they call me the daughter of a street dancer,' Sundri said in a rush, 'Let them say it, let them say it a thousand times.'

'No, Sundri. I don't want this secret of yours revealed. If you truly love me, then let it remain concealed. In any case, the court will never consider your statement to be true. You don't have any evidence to support it.' Bachan Singh paused, looking thoughtful. 'But I wonder why she didn't leave a note?'

'Perhaps she thought she would have had to reveal my relationship to her. Perhaps she didn't want anyone to know that I'm her daughter. And she could never have imagined that her extreme actions would cause you…' Sundri's throat filled up, and she could not speak further.

They had barely had a chance to talk before the bell marking the end of the visit rang out loud. The prisoners left the grill either of their own will or by the kicks of the guards. Sundri's heart was full of sorrow. She wanted to say so much more to Bachan Singh. Darkness overwhelmed her at their separation, and she did not realize when Bachan Singh moved away from her or what his last words to her were.

34

AN AIR OF DEEP, impenetrable gloom hung over Sundri. As far as she could see or imagine, there was nothing except misery. She had sunk into a dream-like state of despair. Since the case was being presented before the court in Amritsar, Giani ji and Sundri stayed there. In any case, it was too risky for Sundri to remain in Rawani or Diwanpur.

It was crystal clear to everyone what the verdict would be – it was impossible for Bachan Singh to escape punishment. His public opposition to Anwarjan's performance was being stated as his motive for the murders, and his presence outside her house on the night of the crime had also been proved – the fake witnesses produced by Pala Singh and his men had confirmed it.

But what had actually happened? That fateful night, after Sundri left Anwarjan, the dancer had sent one of her troupe members to bring Karam Chand and Pandit Radhey Krishan to her house. A special invitation from Anwarjan was nothing less than a heavenly blessing to both of them, and they rushed to meet her. They were both already drunk, and Anwarjan made them drink more. When they both had almost lost consciousness due to alcohol, Anwarjan attacked them with a deadly strike of her knife, killing both on the spot. Later, she turned the same knife to herself and ended her own life.

When Anwarjan's old maid Anna came to the house the next morning, she began screaming in horror. Several people from the neighbourhood rushed inside when they heard her loud shrieks. The entire room was bathed in red, and three bodies were lying in a pool of blood.

When Pala Singh and his men found out about the killings, they jumped with joy. They called the police immediately and presented Bachan Singh as the villain.

No one but Sundri knew the secret behind the deaths. Though almost everyone thought Bachan Singh guilty, they were still unsure initially. Bachan Singh might have killed Anwarjan in a rage for social reform, but why would he kill the other two when he did not have any enmity with them? However, their hesitation quickly evaporated when the witnesses recorded their statements: 'Pandit Radhey Krishan and Karam Chand had gone to Anwarjan's house to discuss the concluding part of her performance. Bachan Singh was there, having killed Anwarjan and holding a blood-stained knife and killed both of them on the spot to avoid any witnesses to his crime.'

Bachan Singh's lawyer had recorded Sundri's testimony as a witness in his favour. Even though she told the court the entire story from beginning to end, it was found irrelevant to the case. Sundri did not have any evidence to support what she was saying. The three people who could have corroborated her story were dead. The only witness to attest to Anwarjan's past was Tara Chand, but no one knew his whereabouts or whether he was even alive. 'If you could manage to find him even at this stage, it might be helpful', the defence counsel told Sundri in despair.

Although Sundri testified that Anwarjan had clearly pledged to kill the two men, she had not actually witnessed the crime. Hence, the court dismissed her testimony.

The one difference Sundri's statement made was that the people who had earlier derisively called her the daughter of an Untouchable now addressed her as the daughter of a whore.

Bachan Singh met Sundri and Giani ji several times as the case progressed, but it might be best not to sadden the reader by presenting those fruitless meetings. The court of law, after all, is a servant of the rich and the master of the poor.

After winding up its proceedings, the session court finally and inevitably awarded the death sentence to Bachan Singh.

Even though Bachan Singh's relatives filed an appeal in the high court, the sentence was too much for Sada Kaur to bear, and the old woman became delirious.

When it came to Sundri, however, the blazing rage of revenge inside her heart did not let her falter. Instead, it only made her tougher.

35

GIANI JI AND SUNDRI were living in a rented house on one of Amrtisar's narrow streets, but all their efforts to save Bachan Singh had proved futile. In her heart, Sundri knew the appeal in the high court was a mere formality. Nothing would come out of it.

With each passing day, she became increasingly anxious about finding Tara Chand, but it was an impossible mission. She was furious with herself for not having asked Anwarjan about his appearance. How could she find him without knowing anything about him? All she had learned from her mother was that Tara Chand used to work in a government office in Sialkot years ago. She spent several days visiting every government office in Sialkot, but this nineteen-year-old clue wasn't enough, and she had to return to Amritsar, sad and dejected.

Still, Sundri did not lose heart. She remained as determined as ever and resumed writing, hoping to earn money. She remained busy from daybreak to nightfall, unconcerned about her health or appearance. She waited for the high court verdict and wrote feverishly during those months. Her articles and stories were published in several Punjabi magazines and created a stir among the readers, making her extremely popular.

Giani ji tried his best to take care of Sundri during this period. He tried to bring her peace with his spiritual words, but the fire inside her could not be appeased. Sundri was becoming weaker by the day, but her heart was fiercer than ever. It seemed she detested the whole world. Her life felt like an intolerable burden.

One day, she received a letter from Bachan Singh. Her heart began to beat faster when she recognized his handwriting. She opened the envelope with shaking hands. 'Sundri, my final love…' she began to read. She reeled at these words but controlled herself and continued reading: The appeal has been rejected, and the day of execution has been scheduled for Tuesday…

The letter fell from Sundri's hand. Trembling, she picked it up again: 'Sundri! Can you imagine my condition right now? This world is a terrible place. Although I am being in a cell – meant not for ordinary prisoners but those awaiting the death sentence – I feel free like I'm watching myself, hovering over this world. Different scenes are flashing before my eyes, one after the other. Everything that I've witnessed since my birth.

My entire view of life changed when the jail superintendent announced the judge's order. The walls of the cell, the roof, the door, the floor, everything was tearing at my eardrums with chants of "Death! death!" The guard walking around my cell block appeared singing the song of my death. The crows sitting on a nearby tree were squawking as if they did not remember any other sound except "death".

I was trembling from head to toe. It was not a physical sensation, but a feeling inside me – my heart, my brain, my thoughts, everything – was trembling. The floor, the roof, the courtyard, the trees – all were trembling.

I remained in that state for several hours. Then, another scene flashed before my eyes. I saw the image of an innocent angel, pale as a sunflower, its body a bundle of bones like a skeleton in a laboratory. But a strange glow was emanating out of that pale face. I felt a deep sense of elation at that image. I forgot that I had been condemned to death. It was my Sundri.

Then the image vanished, and the next moment, my eyes were looking upon the cruel noose. A dark-faced executioner was readying it by polishing the rope with oil. I started trembling again at that horrible sight. It was as if my heart was pleading before the executioner, "Don't be so hasty, my friend. I have many tasks to complete, let me finish them, I won't take much time, I'll be quick..." But the executioner seemed even more in a hurry, "I'm anxious to complete my own task, too, just as you're anxious to complete yours," he said and continued working on the noose.

My heart was saddened to hear his reply. I felt like a traveller who had still not loaded his luggage on the train, but the conductor had already waved the green flag, and the train had given a whistle to depart.

Sundri, I remember you had praised death in one of your

old letters. I had started feeling the same. But today, after hearing about the execution, I've forgotten all your words.

I had asked you not to meet me in the past as it would be too painful for me, but I feel the opposite now. You are the only solution to all my troubles. I want to meet you once, and only once, before I die. I'm sure that will be enough for me to die in peace.

Sundri! Who is writing all this? Where are these whirlpools emerging from? How can a meagre heart absorb all these emotions? And will all these thoughts end abruptly with the single jerk of a 4-metre rope? Will the rivers flowing from these eyes become dry and barren instantly? Will the hand driving this pen at an electrifying speed become as hard as wood within six days from today?

The heavenly idol enthroned in the temple of my heart, whom I worship every day with the flowers of my love – will this model of perfection be shattered to pieces with a single blow of destiny's cruel hammer?

Sundri, I should stop writing now. My woes are never-ending, and a parched man's thirst cannot be quenched by drinking water in his dreams. Our relationship might only have lasted for a short period, but it will endure until the end.

Look, Sundri, I could not understand the meaning of your letter earlier, but now I do. Don't you want to live after my death? I must beg you never to bring any harm to your life. But even if you refuse to agree, I must make you aware of something. From now on, you have the responsibility of taking care of a bereaved soul, my mother, who is languishing between life and death. Until you are free from this responsibility, you have no right to end your life. After all, we will reunite and be together for millions of years. Then why consider this brief separation a difficult one? I'll wait for you, but you cannot come to me until you fulfil the responsibility that I'm assigning to you.

I will be meeting my family on Monday and you the next day. Come here on Tuesday with Giani ji. And Sundri, there won't be any time restraints. The superintendent has promised me this special privilege.

Oh, Sundri, should I finish my letter now? How difficult it is for me. As if with the completion of this letter, my entire world will be finished.

The paper is over; there is no space, not even on the margins. The attendant is asking me to stop writing immediately as the superintendent is about to come.

My dearest, Sundri! I'm closing this letter while keeping your precious face in my mind.

Final love.

Yours,

Bachan Singh

36

A VORTEX OF ENDLESS thoughts had swirled within Bachan Singh in the days following the death sentence. Finally, only two words echoed in his mind: 'hanging' and 'death'.

There was no ebb and flow of emotions in his heart on the day of the hanging. Only the picture of death presented itself before him. He felt as if he had already left this world and gone on to the next. The squeaking of an oil extraction machine in a nearby barrack sounded to him like a widow mourning the death of her husband. The soft sounds of a caterpillar crawling in the corner of his cell felt as if a mother was bitterly crying while holding her dead son in arms. Sometimes, he noticed birds fluttering in the open compound outside his cell, but death seemed to be following them, too – they seemed to be flying in fear.

Locked in his dingy cell in the Lahore Central Jail, he thought about his unfortunate mother, who had come to meet him the previous day. Then he thought about Sundri, who was supposed to meet him today. She must have gotten off the train by now, he thought. Her thin, pale hands would shake while handing her ticket to the ticket collector. She wouldn't even clearly see the way due to the tears in her eyes. Giani ji would console her and help her sit in the tonga. The trees along the side of the road would appear streaming backwards with the movement of the tonga. She would think of them as old memories. 'Go, my friends. Go forever,' she would think. The tonga would reach the jail any moment now. Sundri would first notice the giant black iron gates. They would appear to her as if in mourning. The guard pacing in front of the gate would appear to her as the messenger of death. How would Sundri be able to bear all that?

The sound of heavy boots resounded from outside, and Bachan Singh jumped up. A British superintendent, a doctor, two jail officers, and several policemen were standing outside.

The door of his cell opened, and without anybody saying a word, he understood the time of his execution had come.

He stretched out both his arms, and a policeman handcuffed him. He was made to walk ahead alone while the rest of the men followed him.

Bachan Singh felt as if he were floating. It seemed like his head no longer held his brain, and his chest was without his heart. And yet, a yearning inside jolted him every few moments. His eyes had become as solid as stone, but still, they wanted to see. His fingers touched the chain of the handcuffs to feel if it was iron or flesh.

Finally, he found himself standing at a place he had never seen before but had imagined – the place where he would be executed. His body trembled, and there was nothing but darkness before his eyes.

He was not aware of how long he had been standing

there when he heard a voice, 'Bachan Singh, do you have anything to say?'

Who answered this question? Was it him? He knew he had spoken, but he could not understand his own words. 'All right, call them', another voice said.

He heard someone scream. Recognising the voice, he turned around. It was Sundri, with Giani ji supporting her by the shoulders.

Upon Giani ji's request, Bachan Singh's handcuffs were removed. Giani ji held Bachan Singh's hand in one hand and Sundri's in the other. The two of them faced each other, their eyes fixed on the other. They saw nothing but each other's image in their pupils – it was as if Bachan Singh was hiding inside Sundri's eyes and Sundri in Bachan Singh's.

Sundri felt something around her neck. She noticed Giani ji had unfastened the knot of his scarf, pulled out a garland of flowers and placed it around their necks. He had also placed her hand in Bachan Singh's. Grasping both their hands in his palms, Giani ji spoke, 'O Lord, may the love of this couple last until the end of time and may they spend eternity together in heaven.'

The British officer removed his hat. The other men bowed their heads. '*Ameen*! *Ameen*!' they said in unison.

Bachan Singh and Sundri engulfed each other in a deep embrace. A minute passed, two minutes, five minutes, then ten minutes, but their embrace did not loosen.

Finally, at a gesture from the superintendent, Giani ji spoke up, 'Bachan Singh, Sundri! My children, enough.'

But still, they did not release each other. Finally, Giani ji took Sundri's arm. 'My child', he repeated. The superintendent held Bachan Singh's arm, speaking his name as if to return him to his senses.

The two loosened their arms from around each other. Bachan Singh stood still as if in a daze. A policeman covered his head with a large black hood.

Sundri almost fell unconscious, but Giani ji caught her. The superintendent ordered a bed for her.

When Sundri woke up, the darkness of night had spread everywhere. From the noise of engines, the shouting of passengers, the calls of hawkers, and the smell of cigarette smoke, she realized that she was in the waiting hall of a railway station.

She asked Giani ji for water, and he went to get it for her. The events of the day, which she had forgotten for the briefest of moments, came alive in her mind again. She felt a heaviness in her head. There was no thought, no idea or imagination left. She was like a roof whose supporting pillar had been destroyed.

She remained in a state of complete bewilderment, looking around with dejection. Giani ji returned with some water, and she felt some strength return after drinking it. Her brain awakened.

Her last meeting with Bachan Singh flashed before her eyes like a dream.

He is dead. The moment this thought came to her mind, she let out a wail, covered her face with her hands and lay down on the bench. Several passengers gathered around Sundri, and after being told by Giani ji that her innocent husband had been hanged to death earlier that morning, tried to console her.

Sundri wanted to cry, but she could not. She did not know how to. The flames raging inside her had dried her tears.

She got up and went outside the waiting hall. As far as she could see, passengers milled about her. She scanned them carefully. An odour of deception and malice seemed to emanate from every human being there. She felt everything God had created around her was meant for her destruction. She looked up at the sky. Only a few scattered dark clouds dressed for mourning seemed to share her sorrows. A few stars were twinkling, but unable to bear her grief, they hid behind the clouds.

All of a sudden, an electric surge jolted her. Her eyes flashing with anger, she shouted at the people around her. 'What are you looking at? Aren't you satisfied even after drinking my blood? You've already deprived me of everything. What else can you do? You've ended my master, my world, and still...'

Giani ji grabbed Sundri's arm and tried to get her to sit down. 'My child, please control yourself,' he begged.

Several people edged away from them. Giani ji caressed Sundri's head as he continued in a soft voice. 'My child, you will put your life in danger with such behaviour. What had to happen has...'

Sundri laughed. 'My life in danger? No, I'm not going to die yet. I've got a lot to do, and I won't die before doing it. What about his cremation, Giani ji?'

'It has already been performed. I tried my best to revive you for it but…'

'It doesn't matter anyway.'

When they reached Amritsar and had exited the platform, Sundri turned to Giani ji, 'Giani ji, I don't want to bind you for too long; please leave me alone for a few days.'

'Leave you alone?' Giani ji asked, surprised. 'But why, my child?'

'I'm going to Diwanpur.'

'Why?'

'Bachan Singh gave me the responsibility of taking care of his mother. I will stay with her for a few days.'

'All right, I'll accompany you to Diwanpur then.'

'No, Giani ji, I'll go alone', Sundri insisted.

Despite a long argument, Giani ji had no choice but to agree with Sundri's decision. She would go to Diwanpur, and Giani ji would stay a few more days in Amritsar before returning to Haridwar.

37

AFTER EMERGING FROM THE railway station, Sundri headed toward the road leading to Diwanpur. Her thoughts were more coherent now. She thought of Bachan Singh in each passing moment, but the memory no longer made her cry in anguish. As iron becomes harder with the heat of fire instead of melting or burning, Sundri's heart, too, became stronger after Bachan Singh's death. She did not feel the sting of sorrow as sharply as she had expected. Perhaps her heart had become accustomed to getting hurt.

She reached Diwanpur around 8 p.m. and immediately made her way to Sada Kaur's house. She knocked at the door. A voice came from inside, 'Who is there?'

Sundri answered hesitatingly, '*Bebe* ji! It's Sundri.'

She knew Sada Kaur's words would be harsher than ever. She had insulted her even when Bachan Singh was alive; God only knew the names the old woman would call her now. But she had promised Bachan Singh. She made up her mind to bear it all.

The door opened. Sada Kaur was holding a lamp in her hand. Her eyesight had become too weak to recognize anyone even in daylight. Sundri waited for the inevitable blow, the volley of fireballs that would emerge from her mouth. But to her surprise, Sada Kaur spread her arms wide. 'Oh my unfortunate child, come!'

Sundri fell at her feet. Sada Kaur lifted her and embraced her. '*Beti*, you've become a widow today.'

Sundri could not speak a word and began crying as Sada Kaur told her about the last time she had met her son. Bachan Singh had told her everything about Sundri and had asked his mother to consider Sundri akin to him and to take care of her. And as Sundri, too, shared her sorrow with Sada Kaur, it felt, for a while, as if Bachan Singh was present with them.

They talked till late at night, both wondering how they would have been able to bear their condition without the presence of the other.

Sada Kaur told Sundri she had run out of money. She had been forced to sell her jewellery and mortgage her land to meet the expenses of the trial. Some of the land had already been seized by her relatives, and Sundri found out that Pala Singh was inciting them to steal what was left.

It was yet another blow to Sundri. The flames of revenge inside her raged with greater intensity. Every minute she spent in the house began to feel unbearable, and as soon as Sada Kaur went to sleep, she quietly got up, took a matchbox from a shelf, and left the house.

It was past midnight. Sundri reached the small cottage near the village well where Pala Singh and his men usually gathered. There was a hole in the back wall, through which a part of the cottage was visible. Sundri positioned herself near the hole and peeped inside. A lamp was glowing. She could see Pala Singh with two other men. They were drinking. She heard Veer Singh speaking, 'The enemy has been eliminated, and not one finger has been raised against us.'

Pala Singh spoke, his voice inebriated. 'Did you really see her going to Jeeva Singh's house tonight?'

'I swear by the Guru; I saw her with my own eyes.'

'She cannot escape now. Grab her tomorrow. Let's finish this.'

'But brother, where will you keep her?'

'We have plenty of places to keep her. Just pick her up tomorrow.'

'But brother, she gave a statement in court that she is the daughter of that street dancer.'

'Stop your nonsense. Why do you Sikhs care so much about these things? Just recite the Guru's name and grab her at night. I think we should break through the mud wall at the back of Jeeva Singh's house and...'

Sundri need not listen any longer to understand what they were planning but she waited as the men drank more while plotting, and eventually fell asleep.

In the meantime, Sundri set to work around the cottage, painstakingly gathering three large heaps of dry grass and straw with the intention of setting the cottage on fire and killing those inside.

The flames that soon engulfed the cottage were visible even from a distance. Several villagers ran toward it. Sundri stood near the fire, her mad laughter so loud that it could frighten death itself.

There was chaos everywhere. Some villagers reached the cottage, but before they could even think of rescuing the men inside, the roof collapsed, the dried stacks of wood adding more fuel to the fire.

'She was just here, right here...' some shouted while trying to extinguish the fire. Others started running around in a frenzy, trying to catch the culprit.

A man said he had seen a young girl running toward the river, and several villagers started racing in that direction, trampling the bushes on the way.

'Look there, she's heading to the bridge,' someone shouted.

The villagers rushed toward the bridge. But they could not see anything in the darkness. A voice rang out, 'Come on, catch me if you dare! Yes, I'm a killer. I've taken three lives against two. But I haven't killed anyone innocent. I've killed those who ruined the life of my master and drank the blood of my old father. Do not forget that those who make a woman a widow cannot escape the fire of her rage. God will punish everyone responsible for the execution of my innocent master, those who protected the killers of my father by giving false testimony in the court. Those murderers have been rewarded for their evil deeds. Come on now, catch me!'

Sundri could be seen standing on the bridge, shouting these words, her arms raised in the air.

The police had reached the scene by now. They ran toward the bridge, with the villagers following close behind, wondering why Sundri was not running away from them.

Even when they reached the bridge, Sundri stood still, cursing them at the top of her voice. But as soon as the policemen moved to grab her, she jumped into the river.

There was a loud splash in the smooth river. The water turned frothy and white where she had fallen. Then, there was a complete silence. The crowd shone their lanterns at the river, but could not find Sundri. She had disappeared.

Although everyone had seen Sundri jump into the river, no one could say whether she had drowned or if she had managed to swim safely to the riverbank.

Over the next few days, the police announced a handsome reward for anyone with information about Sundri's whereabouts. A rigorous search was launched, and posters of Sundri's crime were printed and circulated everywhere. But she was nowhere to be found.

38

Concluding Part of the Unfinished Episode

Two years later

READERS KNOW THAT AT the beginning of this book, a passenger named Gupteshwar was reading his handwritten novel to Shyam Das. It was a long novel, but Shyam Das wanted to hear it all in one sitting.

As Gupteshwar read and Shyam Das listened, the night passed, and the day arrived. He had almost finished the entire novel, except for the very end, when the bright golden sunrays entered the room.

Gupteshwar took a few minutes to arrange the remaining pages of his manuscript. The last chapter had been scribbled on whatever he had managed to find – some of it was written on one side of the pages of a school notebook, some on the outer margins of a newspaper.

After arranging the pages in serial order, Gupteshwar looked at Shyam Das. To his surprise, the man was crying.

His face had become pale like a dead man's, and his lips were trembling.

'Sir!' the passenger said, keeping the papers aside, 'Why are you crying? It is not such a great tragedy.'

But the words did not seem to reach Shyam Das's ears and his tears continued to fall.

'I'll keep this conclusion aside for now. In any case, it is still unfinished.'

'No!' Shyam Das said, wiping his tears and regaining control of his emotions. 'Please, continue reading, I'm fine.' He took the writer's hand. 'What a heartbreaking story it is.'

The passenger picked up the rough bundle of pages and resumed reading.

39

GUPTESHWAR WAS KNOWN AMONG his readers only by his name. No one was familiar with his face. He had become quite popular within two years, and publishers and editors were curious to meet him, but his whereabouts remained unknown even after multiple attempts to find him. They received all the material from Gupteshwar only by post, along with a note that mentioned the address where the compensation had to be sent: 'Mrs. Sada Kaur, c/o the late Mr Jeeva Singh, Village Diwanpur, District Amritsar'. They had tried several times to find Gupteshwar by sending letters and even messengers to that address, but no one in the village knew anybody named Gupteshwar. The old woman who received the money never gave them a satisfactory response.

Gupteshwar lived in a small room in the Bhagtanwala locality of Amritsar at a monthly rent of 8 annas. No one ever noticed him interact with anyone. He would lock himself in his small room and write all day. At night, he wandered around the gardens and secluded areas on the city outskirts. The gardeners had noticed him singing and sometimes crying. Some people called him *mast*.

He occasionally walked around in some of the city's

crowded areas, calling out to passers-by and asking them absurd questions. Most of them ignored him and walked away, but a few did stop to talk to him.

There was nothing in his room that conveyed a sense of comfort. In one corner was his bed – a wooden platform covered with a torn rug – and in another was a stove made of three adjoining bricks. A small griddle, an earthen bowl, a platter and some pieces of dried wood and straw were kept nearby. A lamp stood on a brick near his bed. This was what he sat next to and wrote while keeping a small, flat piece of wood on his knees to support his sheets of paper.

Some carriage-repair shops, owned by Muslim blacksmiths, a few handcart-making carpentry shops, and two sweets shops stood near his room.

That day, he had been writing since morning with an old, worn-out blanket wrapped around his knees – the same that he used as his quilt at night. On his right was a heap of waste paper. One side of these papers seemed to have school material scribbled on it, while the other side had turned blue due to the ink having spread.

At dusk, after writing for the whole day, he put his pen aside, took hold of the written sheets and got up. On reaching the door, he stretched his body, straightened his back and twisted his fingers to get rid of the cramps.

After counting the pages, he said, 'Just this chapter, this one concluding chapter; I'll finish the rest today, then I'll be free of this dreadful secretive life. I have not been able to accomplish my second mission, but what can I do? If it is not in my destiny, I can't achieve it. I cannot waste any more time on this peculiar task. I've suffered enough.'

The next moment, an expression of extreme worry appeared on his face as though he were a passenger who noticed his wallet was missing after the train he was on had started moving. The realization of having run out of writing paper caused a similar trepidation within him.

He placed the bundle of papers back where his other handwritten papers were stacked, and lay on his bed with his arm under his head, pulling up his blanket.

One cannot survive without money, and he did not have any. He moved out of his room early in the morning, as desperate as a wingless bird hopping about in search of food. The early morning winter chill had increased his troubles. All he had to save himself from the frigid cold was an odd-sized coat with broken buttons and torn buttonholes. He had used a thick cotton string to keep the coat closed by running one end through the torn buttonholes and tying the other around the buttons. He was wearing half-pants; his legs were bare and covered with dust and grime, like those of coal workers in a railway workshop. The condition of his face and hands was the same, but this grime did not look as bad on his fair-complexioned face. He was not wearing shoes, and there were corns on his bare feet.

He wandered through the streets to find some paper while shivering with cold, but it was all in vain. He became furious with himself and his fate and returned to his room disappointed and dejected. He felt like throwing his incomplete book into the fire and ending his wretched life. He even put this thought into action, collecting all his papers and putting them on the stove. But when he picked up the matchbox, it was empty. This infuriated him even more. He went out of his room in search of a light.

Suddenly, his thoughts made an about-turn. He stood for a long while, supporting his back against the wall outside his room. Then, he re-entered the room, collected all the papers from the stove and put them back from where he had picked them up. Then, he left the room to try his luck once more.

While walking, he thought of a moneylender he was acquainted with. He went to him and asked to borrow one rupee, which he got after promising to repay double.

He went straight home, collected his papers into a bundle, and reached the railway station. After a few hours, he was wandering the markets of Lahore, a web of gloom enveloping him. No one accepted his manuscript – first, on seeing it was a bundle of waste paper; second, on seeing his pitiful condition. A couple of publishers offered him a mere ten to fifteen rupees. Had he told people he was Gupteshwar, they would have touched the ground under his feet to their foreheads, but he could not do that. Like an absconding murderer, he wanted to conceal his identity at any cost.

While returning home, he had just a quarter of a rupee left, and even that was a counterfeit coin. He boarded the train without buying a ticket. A few sheets of newspaper were lying on a seat. He requested a pen from a passenger and started writing the concluding part of his book, but it remained incomplete…

Shyam Das's eyes were wet. He noticed that the papers from which Gupteshwar was reading were actually old newspapers with their outer blank margins filled with handwritten text, so much so that there was no blank space left on any of them. Now, he was holding the last page of the book, the same sheet of newspaper. After reading the lines written in the margins, he stopped and kept the paper on his bed because it was still not finished.

After finishing reading, Gupteshwar glanced at Shyam Das's face, again; it had become very pale. 'I think you're not feeling well because of lack of sleep,' Gupteshwar said to him sympathetically. 'Please rest.'

'No, no, continue reading,' Shyam Das said, taking a deep breath.

'That's all', Gupteshwar replied. 'This is finished, except for the concluding episode that I…'

'Finished?' Shyam Das asked him, suppressing the pain within himself, 'And how much is left?'

'Just a little.' Gupteshwar looked at his troubled face again.

'But Gupteshwar Sahib!' Shyam Das said, 'I beg your pardon, please tell me if this is the creation of your own mind or something—'

Gupteshwar interrupted, 'No, sir, it is based on a real incident I heard about from someone. I have only painted it on the canvas.'

Shyam Das wiped the sweat from his forehead with his handkerchief. 'But could you tell me from whom you heard this story?'

'From Sundri.'

'Really? Did she narrate all this to you herself? Where and when did she meet you?' Shyam Das was nervous while asking this question; streaks of sweat had formed on his body.

'In a village.'

'And you created a novel out of that?'

'Yes, I found the subject very interesting.'

Shyam Das was furious, but he hid his expression. 'Pardon me', he said, 'but a writer of your calibre could have constructed an even better plot out of your own imagination instead of using someone else's real life story.'

'You're right, but I expected more success with this one.'

'I'm sorry, but I'm a straightforward man, and I speak the truth to a person's face. Though your literary genius has won my heart, what you are saying seems wrong. Have you heard this story? Once upon a time, a professional diver was entertaining people by demonstrating his diving skills in a pool of water. In a fit of excitement, and to win the applause of the spectators, he started doing complex somersaults beyond his capacity. He lost control of his breathing, drowned and died on the spot. He remained underwater for quite some time as water entered his lungs. The spectators were amazed at his skills, thinking he was still alive. "Wow! What a great dive! He's still underwater!" they shouted while clapping. After some time, when his swollen dead body resurfaced, they got even more excited, saying how good he was at swimming exactly like a dead man. Similarly, you have taken advantage of the deplorable life of that poor girl, whose every moment was full of misery. Someone has rightly said, "The goat is concerned about life, and the butcher is concerned about meat."

'Gupteshwar Sahib! I'm sorry to say this act of yours puts your reputation under question, depicting your heartlessness. You should have helped that unfortunate girl instead.'

Gupteshwar lowered his eyes and said, 'Yes, it was indeed a big mistake on my part, but my heart compelled me to do so.'

'It is okay, all human beings tend to make mistakes, only God is perfect. It appears that Sundri narrated her story to you just a little before she drowned.'

'Yes, she had told me her story the day before she died.'

'Then how did you come to know about her drowning in the river?'

'I was staying in the same village then.'

Shyam Das felt as if someone was plucking his flesh with pliers. Every vein and every pore of his body was squirming in pain. He said after a pause, 'You've done a remarkable job, Gupteshwar Sahib. I guess you intend to introduce yourself in the capacity of the author in this last episode. Am I right? But do finish the remaining pages today. I request you to stay at my house from now on so that I can spend the remaining days of my life in your company. I hope you won't dishearten me by declining my request. Please tell me more about that destitute girl – as much as you know.'

Gupteshwar replied cordially, 'It would have been a real pleasure for me if I could accept your request.'

'Why? What do you mean?'

'The remaining episode of my own life is still incomplete, just like my novel.'

'What? What did you say? You... you...'

'Yes, I don't have anywhere to live or any more time. I... I...' Gupteshwar paused and, despite repeated questions from Shyam Das, did not complete his sentence.

When Gupteshwar spoke next, he said, 'I need a favour from you.'

'It would be the greatest honour. Please tell me what I can do for you.'

'You truly are like an angel in the garb of a human. I don't have words to express my respect for you.'

Upon hearing Gupteshwar's words, Shyam Das lowered his eyes and said, 'Consider me your servant for the rest of my life. You can ask me to do anything you consider me capable of. But for God's sake, don't use such words to describe me. I'm a cheap, boisterous and undignified person. I've committed heinous crimes in my life. You'll be stunned if you come to know one of them. I am not worth this praise. Such honours are best suited for people like you.'

Gupteshwar's eyes glistened in pity as he heard Shyam Das's words. He bowed his head in gratitude.

'Please give me your orders,' Shyam Das said.

Gupteshwar said, 'First, would you be able to retrieve the scarf that I had given to the waiter at Lahore? He works in a hotel opposite the Lahore Railway Station. Second, if possible, arrange to get this novel published and send the earnings to the address I mentioned.'

Shyam Das's body had become still as wood. His gaze was fixed on Gupteshwar's eyes, and he was silent. Then, as though he were someone returning after wandering down a wrong path, Shyam Das said, 'I'm sorry, I got lost somewhere. What were you saying?'

Gupteshwar repeated both requests.

Controlling the whirlpool of emotions within his mind, Shyam Das said, 'My pleasure. I'll be the happiest person to accept both of these orders. What's the name you read? Sada Kaur? Is she your relative?'

'Yes.'

'Where is your home?'

'At your feet; now that is going to be my residence.'

'I appreciate your kindness, but I meant, where is your ancestral house?'

Gupteshwar began collecting his papers. 'I think you're quite tired now, and you must rest. You will probably have to go to work soon.'

'No, today is Sunday. Anyway, we'll talk sometime later.'

After a while, Shyam Das spoke again, 'Yes, being Sunday, I think I should go and retrieve your scarf. You've already given me the address of that hotel.'

Gupteshwar repeated it, then asked, 'How long have you been living here?'

'It has been seventeen or eighteen years.'

'Then you must have considerable favour in this city.'

'Yes, by your grace, I've got good connections with a number of people here.'

'Then can you help me with the location of a particular man in this city? I've been trying to find him for the last two and a half years but haven't made any progress. You might jeer at me, for I have neither seen him nor do I know anything about how he looks. Had I been familiar with his face, I might have found him by now.'

Shyam Das said, 'Whatever you know about this man, tell me. I will try my best. I happen to meet various people since I work in the railways department. Tell me whatever you know about him.'

Gupteshwar said, 'I only know his name, nothing else.'

'What is it?'

'Tara Chand.'

'Hello... sir?' Gupeshwar said, looking at Shyam Das. 'What happened? I suppose this lack of sleep is affecting your health again. I think we shouldn't talk about these things any more right now. I advise you not to go to Lahore either. We'll think about the scarf sometime later. Please rest for now. You've become so pale.'

Shyam Das wiped his forehead with a handkerchief and cleared his throat. 'Don't worry,' he said, 'sometimes I become jittery, but it will pass. Which village did Tara Chand originally belong to?'

'He belonged to Sialkot...' Gupteshwar looked at his companion's reaction and continued, 'Sir! Your voice is shaking, please go and rest!'

Shyam Das's anxiety was increasing with each passing moment. Fanning himself with his handkerchief, he said, 'Oh… yes! I know him very well.' His features had become like those of a corpse. His hands were cramping, and his breathing was laboured, like a patient stricken with tuberculosis.

'You do? You know him well?' Gupteshwar said these words with the anticipation of someone suddenly finding a lost treasure. He got up quickly in a fit of excitement and paid no heed to Shyam Das's worsening condition. 'Please tell me quickly where he lives. Can you arrange a meeting with him?'

Shyam Das widened his eyes. 'Yes, of course. I have good dealings with him.'

Trying to stifle his happiness and curiosity, Gupteshwar asked, 'Where does he live? What does he do?'

'He lives in Lahore and works with a government organization.'

'Please arrange for me to meet him. When can you do this for me?'

'I think I'll bring him along this evening.'

'Oh, my dear Shyam Das! I'm thankful to you a thousand, million and billion times. You've won my heart. You've solved a great problem in my life. Though I understand your tiredness and ill health, I cannot restrain myself from begging you to arrange this meeting, no matter how much trouble you face.'

Later, they went to bed, but neither of them could sleep. In the morning, they ate the breakfast Shyam Das's servant had prepared.

Shyam Das left for Lahore by the 12.15 p.m. train after asking Gupteshwar to finish the novel.

Gupteshwar's countenance was glowing. He had never experienced such joy. Today, he had enough paper, good writing equipment and a better place to live. However, he had nothing left to write. He went to bed after breakfast, but the anticipation of the meeting with Tara Chand did not let him sleep.

He waited several hours, counting the minutes and the seconds, with his eyes glued to the clock on the wall.

Finally, it struck five, and Gupteshwar went for a stroll outside the entrance. His heart pounded faster upon noticing a tonga turning towards the house, but it wasn't anyone he knew. Many tongas came and went as the magnitude of his eagerness increased.

At last, a tonga stopped outside, but it was Shyam Das who alighted from it. Guessing Gupteshwar's disquiet, he said, 'He is on his way.'

Gupteshwar heaved a sigh of relief. 'When will he be here?'

Shyam Das was breathing heavily. He trembled and his face wore a fearful expression. Gupteshwar became worried. 'What's the matter? Are you still feeling ill?'

Shyam Das tried to hide his uneasiness with a forced smile. 'It's nothing. The train was late so I boarded a lorry.

There was an accident on the way; the lorry crashed into a tree, and many passengers got injured. I was not injured, but it was extremely frightening.'

'Please come inside and rest. I'll ask the servant to bring you hot milk and—'

Shyam Das interrupted, 'No, Sir! Don't. I have to return to the railway station. Our general manager is coming, and I have to be present. Here's your scarf.'

Without saying anything further, Shyam Das stepped into a tonga. 'Mr Tara Chand will be here at around 6.15 p.m. Please wait for him here only. I think he must have boarded the 4.45 p.m. train.'

He got into the tonga and it soon disappeared around the corner.

Gupteshwar waited till 7 p.m., but there was no trace of Tara Chand. It was getting dark when he suddenly noticed a tall man standing at the door. 'Is this the residence of Mr Shyam Das?'

Gupteshwar understood. 'Come in. Are you Tara Chand?'

'Yes, sir.' The man followed him in. Gupteshwar gestured towards a chair.

Tara Chand was wearing a large overcoat with the collar upturned, and sunglasses, perhaps due to weak eyes. His turban was tied haphazardly.

Both of them sat opposite each other for some time. Eventually, Gupteshwar broke the silence saying, 'So, you are Tara Chand?'

The man did not speak but nodded instead.

'So it is you I have been wandering in search of? It is to drink *your* blood that I survived until this day?' Gupteshwar's voice got louder, and his eyes flashed red.

Tara Chand remained calm. Sitting in the same position, he said in aserious tone, 'I don't understand what you're saying.'

Gupteshwar was now shaking with anger. He could feel violence rising from every pore of his body. He shouted, 'What did you say, you beast! You don't understand what I'm saying? Fine. I've been searching for you all these years to make you understand what I'm about to say.'

Tara Chand said, 'But may I at least know who you are?'

'Why not?' Gupteshwar said bluntly. 'Do you know a woman named Gurdei?'

'Yes, I know her, but how is she related to you?'

'I've been looking for you all this time to tell you about this relationship. Now, tell me, how was she related to *you*?'

'She was my wife.'

'And where is she now?'

Tara Chand did not answer.

Gupteshwar asked again, 'Do you know anything about her, whether she is dead or alive?'

Tara Chand replied with the same calm demeanour, 'I've heard she is dead.'

'From whom have you heard this?'

Tara Chand remained silent.

Gupteshwar shouted, 'No, you're a liar, you're a devil. You don't know whether she is dead or alive, and you're not bothered to find out. All you know is that you left her in the clutches of death. You don't know what happened to her afterwards.'

Tara Chand was trembling from head to toe now, unable to utter a word.

Gupteshwar leapt from his chair in a thundering rage, clenched his fists and pounced on Tara Chand like a ravenous lion. He seized his throat with one hand and, with the other, gripped his coat by the shoulder. Shaking him forcefully, he shouted, 'You monster! Why don't you speak? Do you think I'm going to spare your life? No power in the world can save you now.'

He continued, 'I'll pierce your chest with this', and drew a sharp, shiny dagger from his coat, 'and drink your blood, and it will finally settle this blazing fire in my heart. I've done an injustice by bringing wickedness like you into the house of a nobleman like Shyam Das, and it will be one more sin to soil this holy place with your blood. But I am confident that when my revered host comes to know about your misdeeds, not only will he pardon me but will laud me for relieving the earth of a monster.

'Speak! Even if you don't tell me anything, you will meet the same end. It is enough for me to know that you are the killer of my mother, the despoiler of her honour. Murderer! If you've got anything to say before you die, speak now. You've got 5 minutes.'

Tara Chand was trembling, his eyes fixed on the ground. He did not respond.

Gupteshwar shouted again in a frenzy, 'You cruel man! A man who deceives an innocent woman, traps her, violates her dignity and still does not feel shame, then deserts her when she is pregnant, forcing her to sacrifice her honour and become a lowly street dancer, such a despicable person does not deserve to live and to be called a human being.

'Does such a devil have the right to remain on this earth? I'm leaving this decision to you. Tell me, is such a criminal supposed to live?'

Tara Chand shook his head.

'Then are you ready to die?'

He nodded.

'All right then, get ready.' Gupteshwar wielded his dagger menacingly, in such a quick motion that anyone in Tara Chand's place would have been terrorized to death.

The room had become dark. Not wishing to miss his target, Gupteshwar lowered his raised hand and turned on the light switch. He also locked the door so that Tara Chand could not escape.

When the room was lit up, he saw Tara Chand unbuttoning his shirt with trembling fingers. He was surprised at this; it appeared as if the man was already prepared to die. Gupteshwar did not think it wise to wait any further. He raised the hand holding the dagger and pounced at Tara Chand with electrifying speed as if he wanted to kill him with a single strike. But before his hand could reach Tara Chand's chest, Gupteshwar's eyes fell upon his face.

His hand lowered, and he stepped forward to get a closer

look. Tara Chand's turban had unraveled, and his sunglasses had fallen off. When Gupteshwar touched him, he was drenched in sweat and cold as ice.

Gupteshwar cried out and stepped away. He felt darkness swim before his eyes. He removed Tara Chand's sunglasses and said in a shocked voice, 'Shyam Das?'

The entire room seemed to be revolving before Gupteshwar's eyes. Nothing made sense. He stared at the man he had thought was Tara Chand. The dagger fell from his hand.

Gupteshwar was embracing Tara Chand – it was an unfathomable meeting of a father and daughter.

Holding her tight and weeping, Tara Chand said, 'My Sundri! The unfortunate daughter of a cruel father!'

He noticed something on the floor and grabbed it. The next moment, the dagger was in his hands. Tara Chand pointed it towards himself. It would have pierced his chest and touched his backbone if Sundri had not held it with both her hands forcefully.

Tara Chand's hands were shaking like a candle flame battling a strong wind. He heard a loving voice say, 'Baba! Don't take such a step. Whatever was destined has already happened.'

'Sundri, my child! Forgive me! Forgive your cruel father, not by keeping him alive, but by killing him. My child, being alive and living with you is a thousand times worse than dying. I appeared before you this way so that you could complete my punishment. Be quick, and don't make the burden of my sins heavier by keeping me alive in such a condition. You must fulfil the wishes of your unfortunate mother, otherwise, her soul will wander forever, and you will be responsible for that.'

Sundri, not Gupteshwar, but Sundri, now helped him sit on his bed and wrapped her arms around his neck. 'My mother had assigned me the task of killing a man. This task is now complete because that person was dead even before I could kill him. All his bad habits and sins have vanished one after another, and he is leading a life of virtue.'

Tara Chand was sobbing while hiding his face with his hands. Sundri sat beside him. Moving her hand over his forehead, she said, 'Baba, may you live long! I still need you.'

He could not utter a word. Sundri said again, 'Father! Get up and give me your blessings! I'm your own Sundri! Love me as much as you can.'

Tara Chand kissed Sundri's forehead while crying but still could not speak.

Both looked at each other for quite some time as if the eyes were their only means of communication. 'Had you recognized me?' Sundri finally asked.

Tara Chand controlled himself. 'Not completely, my child, but I had suspected your identity. And when you talked about the scarf, my suspicion became certainty. When you asked me where I lived, I looked into your eyes and became sure Gupteshwar was none other than Sundri. And when I saw that scarf, everything became clear to me.'

Sundri recalled that after Bachan Singh was hanged,

she had crocheted the words 'The last remembrance of an unfortunate Sundri's lost crown' on a corner of the scarf.

Tara Chand continued, 'My child! I knew we would soon be introduced the moment I arrested you at the railway station. While looking into your eyes for the first time, the image of your mother reflected before me. Her eyes were exactly like yours. I saw your mother in your eyes yesterday after nineteen years.'

'Sundri', he continued, 'you did not mention this scarf in your story.'

Sundri lowered her eyes. 'Didn't I tell you that once Bachan Singh came to Baba Rodu's cottage where I used to live? It was the day when our monkey, Lachho, was lost. When I was crying, he wiped my tears with this scarf. I have preserved it since then. It is his only…' Sundri's eyes filled with tears, and her voice choked.

Tara Chand said with a gasp, 'But, my child! You've written that Sundri drowned after jumping into the river.'

'Yes, I was drowning, but I didn't die. An old sailor saved me while I was drifting in the river. He was a good man.'

'And then you came to Amritsar?'

'Yes, father.'

'But why did you change your identity?'

'There were several reasons. First, I was concerned about getting caught by the police, for I had committed three murders. Second, I was bound to keep Bachan Singh's promise of caring for his mother. I wanted to earn enough money from my writing to look after her. Third, I wanted to write about the contaminated blood of our society through my autobiography, separate from my other writings. And the fourth mission was to find you and to…' She paused and lowered her eyes.

Tara Chand placed his hand over her head and said, 'Sundri, now you've accomplished all your missions.'

Sundri was quiet for a while. 'Yes, Baba, I'm free of all my burdens now.'

'I want you to be with me always; will you do that?'

'Yes, I'll always remain with you while I live.'

Tara Chand said lovingly, 'I'll go and get some lovely suits stitched for my child. I'd like you to change your attire at the earliest.'

'Yes, I'll be in my true form tomorrow.'

'I'll be so happy to see that! My child, what about the incomplete chapter?'

'It will be before you tomorrow morning.'

After a brief pause, Sundri said, 'Baba, but you haven't told me anything about yourself.'

'*Beti*, my past deeds are so sinful and deceitful that I cannot explain them. Thank God I haven't told you anything. All I can say is that after leaving your mother in the jaws of death and taking all the valuables from the house, I came here. After struggling for some time, I got a job in the railways. It was a mere chance that the railway employees were protesting and going on strikes during that time. Train services were at a standstill. The rail department started hiring to ensure smooth functioning, and I got a job. I changed my name to avoid the hassles of my dreadful past. I was afraid of getting caught.'

Later, Tara Chand went to the market and bought Sundri some suits. Both talked all night, sharing their joys and sorrows, before finally going to bed.

The next morning, when Shyam Das went to Sundri's room, he noticed she was still asleep, wearing her new suit. He called her several times and then shook her, but she did not respond. He removed the sheet from her face and recoiled in shock. Sundri was lying dead in her bed. Her face was glowing with a heavenly light, and there was a smile on her lips. She had placed the scarf on her chest and held it like a lover hugging their beloved at the time of their final separation. Since the scarf was dark red, Tara Chand did not notice at first that it was stained with blood. Then he saw the handle of the dagger beneath the scarf – the rest buried in Sundri's chest.

Tara Chand moaned out loud and started sobbing bitterly. He noticed some papers lying on the table near the bed. It was her last letter:

My respected father, I know you are a courageous man with spiritual knowledge. I'm going away from you – it won't be a small shock, but Baba, after trying to understand my condition, I hope you will regain some peace of mind.

You can well imagine how I have spent these past two and a half years without my other half. His wishes have been powerful enough to keep me alive until now; otherwise, it would have been impossible for me to take a single breath after being separated from him.

But, Baba, despite all this, I'm repentant. I've committed a sin – not a mere sin but a disobedience of the order from my master as well. God will surely punish me for this, and I'm not certain whether my master will forgive me or not.

I have committed the sin of killing Pala Singh and his henchmen. I had gone mad; anger and violence had blindfolded my senses. Bachan Singh had tried his best to steer me towards the right path, and I had made up my mind to keep aggressive thoughts away from my mind, but I was swayed and thought of "an eye for an eye" as the only solution to my pain. But Baba, today I realized that the best form of revenge is the one I've taken from you, the way your life has drastically changed after reading my writings. I could have used the same weapon instead and helped them and others follow the right path.

But time, once gone, does not return. My dear father! Pray that the Almighty has mercy on me.

I was directed by my master not to come to him until I fulfilled my responsibility of taking care of his mother. Since I've found you, I've become free of this responsibility; now it's your duty to take care of her.

At the same time, I'm freeing myself of my mother's responsibility, too. I'm sure that her soul, which yearned to be pacified with your blood, will now be more at peace with your tears instead.

I had one more responsibility – to write my story in the form of a novel – to present the ruthless society before the world. This task has also been accomplished. I am now sacrificing my life and going to live at the feet of my master.

My dear father! You told me last night that you would be glad to see me in my true form. I'm sure you'll keep your word and feel that happiness.

I will not be fortunate enough to bask in the affection of my father, but Baba, my life would have been like a train with no engine. How many blows can a broken heart bear? I'm a murderer on the run. I would rather take my own life with a knife rather than die by hanging.

I promised to stay with you while I was alive. See? I've fulfilled that promise. You asked me several times to complete my writing. My novel and my life are in fact one single entity. Therefore, with its completion, the remaining part of my life has also concluded.

My respected father, bless me so I may embrace my master in heaven and forget the long sorrows of separation.

This is the final wish of your daughter after meeting you for the first and last time.

Yours,
Sundri

ALSO AVAILABLE FROM HACHETTE INDIA

The Starved

Mangalu Charan Biswal
translated by Nirjharini Tripathy

A layered portraiture of Dalit oppression and ruthless hierarchies in 1980s Odisha

Set against the bucolic landscape of undivided Sambalpur, *The Starved* follows five Bajnias – professional rural folk performers – whose lives are pushed into a corner by poverty, social discrimination, addiction and illiteracy. Believed to be conduits connecting ordinary people to the divine, the musicians echo the voices of the gods through the rhythmic play of their instruments. But the decline in folk music and drying farmlands soon become a persistent reality, and the circumstances of those on the fringes devolve from difficult to dire.

Mangalu Charan Biswal's play highlights both the insidious and immediate violence of generational enslavement and casteism, and the wilting landscape of folk art and music. A tale of crippling deprivation and staggering optimism, this revolutionary work of Sambalpuri literature inspects the longevity of hope in the face of adversity and casts a steely gaze on the institutional betrayal of the underprivileged in the country.

ISBN 978-93-93701-81-7

ALSO AVAILABLE FROM HACHETTE INDIA

The Helicopters Are Down

Indira Parthasarathy

translated by Andy Sundaresan

Hurtling towards a midlife crisis, Amirtham is down – but not out.

Caught in a sorry vortex of self-denial and what-could-have-been, the discontented government official wants to do the impossible – be young again. Having decided that his marriage is sparkless and his spouse unremarkable, he decides to woo a much younger theatre actress who vaguely resembles his witty and opinionated ex. As Amirtham gives into self-aggrandizing visions – glamorizing a humdrum life coming apart at the seams – he flails and fails in the tangles of his own making.

In this deeply insightful novel, both endearing and heartbreaking, urban Delhi of the early seventies is brought alive by Tamil literary icon, Sahitya Akademi fellow and Padma Shri-awardee Indira Parthasarathy. Hilarious, reflective and wise, this moving tale expertly courses through unsettling remorse, directionless passion, and the fragile business of loving and being loved.

ISBN 978-93-93701-83-1